Sarah Doudney

A Romance of Lincoln's Inn

Vol. 1

Sarah Doudney

A Romance of Lincoln's Inn
Vol. 1

ISBN/EAN: 9783337066949

Printed in Europe, USA, Canada, Australia, Japan

Cover: Foto ©Andreas Hilbeck / pixelio.de

More available books at **www.hansebooks.com**

BY

SARAH DOUDNEY

AUTHOR OF

"THROUGH PAIN TO PEACE," "WHERE THE DEW FALLS IN LONDON,"

"WHERE TWO WAYS MEET," "GODIVA DURLEIGH,"

"A CHILD OF THE PRECINCT," ETC.

> "And this is an old fairy tale of the heart.
> It is told in all lands, in a different tongue;
> Told with tears by the old, heard with smiles by the young.
> And the tale to each heart unto which it is known
> has a different sense. It has puzzled my own."
> "LUCILE." BY OWEN MEREDITH.

> "Nay," said Sir Dinadan, "for the joy of love is too short,
> and the sorrow thereof, and what cometh thereof, dureth
> over long." MORTE D'ARTHUR.

IN TWO VOLUMES—VOL. I

London 1893

HUTCHINSON & CO.

34 PATERNOSTER ROW

PRINTED AT NIMEGUEN (HOLLAND)
BY H. C. A. THIEME OF NIMEGUEN (HOLLAND)
AND
TALBOT HOUSE, ARUNDEL STREET
LONDON, W.C.

CONTENTS

A ROMANCE OF LINCOLN'S INN.

CHAPTER I.

THE FIRST MEETING.

"Behold her there,
As I beheld her ere she knew my heart,
My first last love; the idol of my youth."

TENNYSON.

IT was half past ten o'clock on a Sunday morning in July—a smiling, old-fashioned July, bringing the rustle of the good green-wood to the feverish heart of London. There was such a whispering of leaves, and quivering of shadows, in the quiet precincts of Lincoln's Inn that Mayne Comberford, stepping out of a house in

New Square, could hardly believe that his country home was many a mile away.

"Here she comes," he said to himself.

The square was as still as if an eternal Sabbath had reigned there for ages. Only three persons were to be seen, a young lady and two children, who had just entered the enclosure from Lincoln's Inn Fields. They were walking slowly; the girl, with a child on her right and left, carried her sunshade with rather a languid air, and glanced about her with the manner of one who took but a faint interest in her surroundings. The children, a boy and girl, seemed to have been laid under a spell of quietness.

But there was, apparently, something in the aspect of this indifferent young woman which made Mayne Comberford quicken his steps. As he drew nearer to her the little boy's tongue was suddenly unloosed; he opened a pair of blue eyes very widely, and began to speak with a queer contortion of his rosy face.

"Loo—loo—loo—look——" he stuttered, and was immediately silenced by the girl's sweet voice.

"Be quiet, Robby. You must not speak at all unless you speak slowly. Never be in a hurry."

"B—b—b—but——"

"Naughty boy," came from the smart little miss on the other side of the governess.

"Hush, Louie, I won't allow you to scold him," said that dignified young person with great decision. "Ah,—Mr. Comberford?"

He had lifted his hat, and was standing before her with a deferential look. How wonderfully pretty she was! Angela's description had not prepared him for anything as lovely as this; but then Angela, poor girl, had never possessed the power of describing beauty.

And, indeed, how could mere words do justice to this soft, brown-tinted face, or give the faintest idea of the deep brown eyes, richly fringed with black lashes? At nineteen Nelly Stanley looked the girl that she was; her lithe figure showed to perfection in a plain suit of pale grey; her dark hair curled rebelliously under a tiny bonnet adorned with one scarlet flower; she had never been dressed more simply even in her school-days.

"It is a great pleasure to meet you at last, Miss Stanley," said the young man, with a certain old-world courtesy which sat very well upon him. She looked up into the honest blue eyes which met hers frankly, yet gravely.

"Angela used to speak of you very often," she said softly, her bright-red lips trembling a little.

"Yes," he answered, "she gave me more love than I deserved. And I miss her more than words can tell."

"I shall never cease to miss her," Nelly remarked, in a low voice. "People laugh at the friendships of school-girls, but they don't realize that such friendships may influence one's life-time. Angela was so good—so unselfish."

"Too unselfish," he replied. "She was afraid of giving pain to those around her, and would not let us know how ill she was."

"It was just like her always: she never complained. I want to hear all about those last days, Mr. Comberford," said Nelly, in a soft, pleading tone. "We will go into the gardens, and sit down for a little while under the trees."

The children, who had been listening to the conversation with all their might, now ran on ahead, and turned in at the gate which opened on the broad gravelled walk. Long afterwards, amid other scenes and under other skies, Mayne Comberford recalled the aspect of these gardens on this quiet Sunday morning. The stillness was intense; stately walls and towers were wrapped in a sunshiny calm; a flock of pigeons, alighting on the gravel as softly as a fall of snow flakes, scattered themselves over the granite steps leading up to the Hall; spaces of green sward were chequered delicately with shadow patterns of the boughs overhead. It was a sweet silent place, almost as peaceful now as in the days when Ben Jonson sang its praises, and Isaac Bickerstaff paced its walks in tranquil meditation.

They sat down on a bench under the shade of the trees. The delicious murmur of the summer foliage was over their heads, and the quietness of the spot enfolded them in its cloister-like seclusion. Robby and his sister were watching the pigeons a little way off; and these two, who had met to-day for the first time, were left alone.

There was a moment of silence in which Mayne Comberford looked earnestly at the face by his side. He noted the " down falling eyelids, full of dreams and slumber," and the brown glow shining under "the shade perpetual" of the jet-black lashes. Everything about this girl was dainty and refined; every feature was delicately moulded; the bloom on the smooth cheek was as rich and soft as the colouring of a chestnut-blossom. What sweet possibilities, half hidden, half revealed, one could find in this rare face! In that brief, silent moment Mayne felt the first heart-throb of the great feeling which was to shape and dominate his future life.

"I had a note from Angela, about a fortnight before she died," said Nelly, in her sad, sweet voice. "The handwriting was faint, and she wrote in pencil. She was a little weak,—a little tired,—she said; but her strength would come back with the summer. I did not even dream that the end was near!"

"If I had known," Mayne spoke under his breath, "I should never have left her for an hour! But I went out one morning, and came back at night to find her dying."

"And she told you to write to me?" Nelly half-whispered.

"Yes." He looked away across the sunlit sward. "It was just at the very last. I saw her lips moving, and bent over her to catch the words,—'write to Nelly,—my love.' I promised, and then she smiled, and was still."

There was another pause. Mayne did not glance at his companion, but he heard her quick breathing. Just then Robby, bursting with a grievance, came running up to the silent couple on the bench.

" Lou—Lou—Lou—" he began, and then stopped short with staring blue eyes, and rosy mouth open. " Wh—wh—what have you m—m—made her cry for?" he demanded of Mayne in a stuttering passion, shaking a stout little fist in the young fellow's face.

" She—she—she cried of her own accord," said Mayne, with great earnestness. " It's n—n—no fault of mine."

" Why—you—stutter—as—bad—as—me ! " remarked Robby, bringing out his words with unusual deliberation. " You should never speak in a hurry, you know."

"I don't often," answered Mayne gravely. "But I can't help it when I'm agitated. You see, you upset me dreadfully."

Robby had gone close to Nelly, and was resting one hand on her shoulder. There was something protecting in the attitude of this sturdy little man in knickerbockers, something chivalrous and true in the blue eyes, that went to Mayne's heart.

The girl looked up at her small champion with a smile, although the tears were trembling on her long lashes.

"I'm all right, Robby," she said. "Don't be concerned; Mr. Comberford has been telling me about a dear friend of mine who is dead."

"About Miss Angela Comberford?" asked Louie, with an inquisitive look. She had joined the group under the trees.

"Yes; this is Mr. Comberford, her brother. Louie, it must be nearly eleven o'clock; don't get hot and flushed before you go into chapel."

"My cheeks feel quite cool," returned the little girl, patting them with a self-satisfied air. "Robby, the big pigeon's come back again; I got quite close to it a minute ago."

Having assured himself that no harm was likely to befall his governess, Robby started off to inspect the big pigeon; and Mayne and Nelly were alone once more.

"Angela told me that you were happy with the Camdens," he said. "And it is clear that you have won the children's hearts;—well, that bonny little fellow is worth winning."

"The world would feel very cold and empty without Robby," admitted Nelly, with a sigh. "A girl in my position cannot expect to make many friends. I have not a single relation; I do not even know if my name is my own. Did Angela tell you my story?"

"She said that you were an adopted child," Mayne replied. "But she did not enter into details. Your history mattered very little to her; she loved you, simply and entirely, for your own sake."

"And I loved her; I can never, never say how well I loved her!"

Her beautiful face, uplifted to his, was glorious with the light of an intense feeling. For a second she was transfigured; the girl had suddenly become a noble woman, with truth and devotion shining in her brown eyes. His heart began to throb fast again; he was not yet in love, perhaps, but very near it, for he was actually saying to himself that he had found his Ideal.

The chapel bell sounded at that moment, breaking upon the sweet calm of the morning, and coming with a brazen clash on the brain. Nelly rose at once; the half-hour under the trees was at an end.

"What a brute of a bell!" said Mayne, in a tone of savage disgust.

"It was taken by the Earl of Essex at Cadiz,

and I wish, with all my heart, that he had left it there!" cried Nelly fervently. "Is there anything more that you want to know about Lincoln's Inn? I am as good as a guide-book. All the Camdens are of the law, legal; and I have to instruct Louie and Robby in the history of the place."

"My head won't stand any more at present, thank you," confessed Mayne, as they passed out of the gardens. "We part here; but you will tell me when I may call on you?" he added, in a voice of entreaty.

"Yes, I will write," she said, giving him her hand.

He stood and watched her slender grey figure until she had vanished into the chapel with her two charges. Then he followed, and a dignified verger was gracious enough to put him into one of the carved oaken pews, not far from Nelly.

Perhaps he was in an impressionable mood

that morning; certain it is that he found himself
quieted and subdued by the spell that was cast
over him here. The colours of the rich stained
windows ("those harmless, goodly windows"
for which Archbishop Laud had trembled in
his day,) rested the eye, and filled the place
with a softened glow. And then came mellow
organ-notes and sweet choral voices which
seemed to answer Milton's prayer, and "keep
in tune with heaven."

Mayne could see Nelly, standing up in one
of the chancel pews set apart for the barristers,
with Robby's fair curly head at her elbow. He
was in a dream, and the light that surrounded
her face was like dream-light, soft and dim.
The voice of the preacher, reading the first lesson
for the day, arrested his wandering thoughts,
compelling him to listen; and that clear tone
drew his attention to the words that were
destined to echo in his heart through years to
come.

" I am distressed for thee, my brother Jonathan; very pleasant hast thou been unto me; thy love to me was wonderful, passing the love of women. "

What should David, the passionate Eastern king, know of the love of women? Through Mayne's fancy there trooped a shadowy procession; Michal, Ahinoam, Abigail, and that Bathsheba who was won by a grievous sin,—these and others, a band of phantoms, toys of the warrior monarch of Israel. And then he looked again at the sweet face which he had seen to-day for the first time.

Could anything pass the love of such a woman as he believed her to be? He recalled her voice and eyes when she had expressed such pure devotion to the dead Angela, her school-friend. If she had loved his sister so well, how deep and strong would be another kind of love when once awakened in her heart. And if he were fated to win so rich a boon

how safely he might trust in her, knowing no
fear of change or falseness or decay!

When the service was over he went out
of the dim chapel into the blazing sunshine,
returning to his silent room. From the window he
looked down upon the empty square, the sunlit
buildings with their varying lights and shades,
the pigeons with their soft grey plumage. Surely
there was romance in the very atmosphere of
this quaint old place, and he was thrilled with a
sense of coming delight.

Yet it was strange how those words haunted
him; they rang in his ears with a mournful
cadence, borrowed from the preacher's tuneful
voice:—"passing the love of women."

CHAPTER II.

MR. COTTRELL'S SECRETARY.

With thy hands go and do thy duty,
And thy work will clear thine eyes.
　　　　　　GEORGE MACDONALD.

SEABERT LAURICE was a barrister who occupied
rooms in a corner house in New Square,—the
corner that is near the chapel. It was a house
that was sure to attract the notice of the few
sight-seers who ever strayed into these deep
solitudes. Scarlet geraniums brightened the
little bit of ground in front; and the branches
of a fig-tree clung to the old wall, and framed the
windows with broad green leaves.

Laurice had gone away on Saturday, and was
expected to return on Monday. Mayne Comberford was the barrister's guest; and as he sat
at breakfast in the empty room on Monday
morning, he missed his friend.

Mayne was still a very young fellow, and youth longs to pour out its experiences to friendly ears. There were a hundred things that he wanted to talk about. It was pleasant to think that Laurice would come home in the evening, and then all his affairs could be discussed over a quiet pipe.

First of all he desired to make it plain that old Cottrell was a trump,—a little mad, possibly, but a trump for all that.

Old Cottrell was Mayne's godfather, and nothing generous had ever been expected of him since Mayne's infancy. On the christening day he had presented his godson with a highly deceptive morocco case, which caused the heart of the proud mother to beat with hope. When the case was opened, its contents were surveyed at first with eyes well-pleased ; but on a closer inspection the fork and spoon, embedded so regally in purple velvet, were found to be plated.

Years passed away; the baby, who had been so blissfully unconscious of that early insult, grew up to be a fine boy, and was even heard to say that old Cottrell was not half a bad fellow. But Mrs. Comberford could not forgive the base deception which had been practised upon her. Women never forget these things; —especially good women of the motherly sort; —and Mayne's mother preserved the morocco case in a drawer, opening it three or four times a year to keep her resentment warm.

Other years came and went, and sorrow entered the pleasant old home among the Sussex downs.

Mayne, the only son, and heir of the Comberford estate, had been brought up with the notion that he was to be a country squire, and live as his father and grandfather had lived before him. But the merry days of Sir Roger de Coverley will never return to the sadder and wiser children of this generation; and Mayne's hopes and dreams were shut up between the brown covers of the old *Spectator*. Nowadays, when he opens those musty volumes, he recalls a vision of the enthusiastic boy who believed himself destined to be a reviver of the past.

"'T were long to tell, and vain to hear" how Mr. Comberford's money had taken wings and fled away. He had never been a rich man, to begin with. Smarting under sundry agricultural disappointments, he had begun to dabble in stocks and shares; and then, just after Angela's death, there came the inevitable result of rash investments.

The eldest daughter was gone; but there were four little girls to be educated and provided for; and the dear old house must be kept over their heads. It was not a mansion, but simply a country home, hallowed by sacred associations, and built in the substantial fashion of bygone days. If the Comberfords had left it, and gone elsewhere, they could hardly have found a

cheaper dwelling-place; it was best to stay on
in the old spot, among the people who knew
and loved them, and the friends who would
not sneer at their economy. They had the
courage to say—"we are poorer than we were
once;"—and this is the kind of courage that
seldom fails to win respect, even in a cynical
world.

At two-and-twenty Mayne suddenly woke up
to the consciousness that he must earn some
money. But how? Wild thoughts of turning
into a sort of Buffalo Bill floated through his
brain; he rode quite well enough to be a cow-
boy, he said to himself. But this idea did not
find favour with his father and mother; and
it was a relief to every one in the house when
old Cottrell wrote to say that he was coming.

Old Cottrell was acquainted with the family
misfortunes, and they all felt sure that he had
a plan for his godson.

They were right. Mr. Cottrell had a plan.

He was an extraordinary old man; but he really had a liking for Mayne.

The guest-chamber in the old house was prepared for his use, and even Mrs. Comberford was ready with a warm welcome. He explained the purpose of his visit on the very first evening after his arrival, and strengthened the family conviction that he was mad,—quite mad. But, as his hostess remarked confidentially to her husband, it was a providential madness so far as Mayne was concerned.

Mr. Cottrell was a barrister; but he had never held a brief, and had devoted himself, all his life, to literary pursuits,—fruitless labours, as his friends were accustomed to say. And now that he was well stricken in years his health was as sound as ever, but his sight was beginning to fail. He wanted an intelligent secretary to prepare his manuscripts for the press; write and answer letters, and bear him company in his lonely hours. He was engaged in writing an exhaustive work on the occult sciences.

"I have given up my house in Kensington," he said. "Now that my daughter has married and gone to India, I have no need of a house. So I shall go back to my old chambers in Lincoln's Inn Fields which chance to be vacant. You shall have two hundred a year, Mayne, if you will come to live with me."

The offer was readily accepted. As Mayne said to his parents, it might prove to be a stepping-stone to something better. Mr. Cottrell had arranged to spend August at the seaside; but he requested his godson to go up to town in July, to inspect the chambers in Lincoln's Inn Fields, and see that all his instructions to the workmen were duly carried out. The rooms were out of repair; Mr. Cottrell was a fidgety man, determined that his wishes should be scrupulously regarded;—and there was a good deal to be done.

Mayne at once decided to go to Seabert Laurice for a day or two. He was not too much occupied with his own affairs to remember the last injunctions of his sister Angela concerning her school-friend. It was in the early summer that Angela had passed away, and every word of hers was still fresh in the hearts of those who had loved her.

"You know, mother, one doesn't expect to meet any one but a very ordinary school-girl," he had said to Mrs. Comberford. "Our Angela, in her goodness of heart, always turned her geese into swans. But this poor little thing is alone in the world, and I shouldn't feel comfortable if I didn't see her, and give her the books and things that Angela wanted her to have."

"See her by all means," Mrs. Comberford replied. "My dear girl was devoted to her. The romantic attachment used to amuse me sometimes," added the poor mother with tears in her eyes. "But it seems sacred now."

So Mayne wrote from Lincoln's Inn on
Friday, asking when he might have the pleasure of calling on Miss Stanley? And Miss
Stanley informed him, by return of post, that
she was coming to the chapel with her pupils
on Sunday morning.

She came, she was seen, and she conquered.

It had struck those friends, who knew him
best, as strange that Mayne's highly-imaginative
spirit had not hurried him into many love-
affairs. But he had evolved for himself an
ideal; none of the pretty girls of his acquaintance had ever lured him away from his shadow-
worship; and he had scarcely even felt such
touches as "are but embassies of love." And
now, as he told himself a thousand times, she
had come; the goddess, long dreamed of, and
waited for; the world was a new place, and
life had only just begun.

Is it always thus that the *belle passion* begins?
Not always; but Mayne's heart was an empty

shrine; and Nelly was as much like a divinity
as it is possible for a mortal to be. She came
surrounded by a halo of romance and tenderness;
and she was, moreover, a most glorious surprise.
Poor Angela, in her enthusiastic affection, had
made Nelly almost ridiculous in the eyes of the
Comberfords; and had quite failed in convincing
them that the wonderful Miss Stanley was at
all a remarkable being. They had listened, with
quiet smiles of incredulity, to rapturous and
vague descriptions of this paragon, and had
glanced with good-natured contempt at a very
bad photograph of her much praised face. The
remembrance of that dreadful portrait had been
in Mayne's mind when he had written his first
note to his sister's friend.

But could any portrait, of any beauty of the
past or present, be more hideously unlike the
original? As Mayne sat at his solitary breakfast
he suddenly bethought him of the "carte"
which he had carelessly slipped into his pocket-

book. He took it out, gazed at it with mutterings of irrepressible disgust, and then fell to wondering if there lived an artist capable of doing justice to Nelly's loveliness?

Angela had been right after all. The poor dead girl, whose opinions had always been lovingly slighted in her family circle, was not the affectionate noodle that her friends believed her to be. With keen self-reproach, Mayne recalled the good-natured sarcasms which he had levelled at his gentle, impressionable sister in days gone by. He wished that she could come back, if only for an hour, to hear his praises of her idol. No listener could be half as patient and sympathetic as Angela; how strangely he had undervalued her good qualities when they had been always together!

Well, Seabert would be at home to-night; and he could talk to Seabert, who was really the best fellow he had ever known. Meantime there was a good deal to be done; and if he was to do his godfather's bidding he must not sit dawdling over cold coffee and bacon.

Two hundred a year! It would be far too small an income for a man to marry upon; although that idiotic little curate, in the Sussex village, had married on a hundred and fifty. The foolishness of curates was inconceivable; but at this moment Mayne was distinctly conscious that he viewed their reckless folly in a new and kindly light.

Out of doors there was the broad sunshine of July, tempered by the softest of summer breezes. The quiet square began to show faint signs of life. Mayne went out through the stately gateway into Lincoln's Inn Fields, and heard the music of many leaves as the light wind stirred the old trees. Workmen were busy about the large house which was to be old Cottrell's home; a ladder was planted against the wall; paint-pots stood upon the doorsteps. Mayne entered at the open door, and ran lightly up a flight of stone stairs to inspect the chambers.

Mr. Cottrell had taken four rooms on the first floor. The dining-room, spacious and lofty, had a bay window overlooking Lincoln's Inn Fields; the walls were covered with a sunny paper. A door opened into the study, which was nearly as large, but far less cheerful. Yet it was in this sombre room that Mr. Cottrell meant to spend the greater part of his time; here he would sit with his books and manuscripts; and here Mayne was to work quietly with the old man, hour after hour, while the great world went its noisy way out of doors, and people laughed and wept, quarrelled and loved.

At that moment the young fellow's heart suddenly sank within him; and he was more than half inclined to call himself a fool. Had he not taken up work for which he was not fit? He began to fear that the hours spent in this dim room would be almost intolerable. It seemed to him that he could not grow accustomed to his drudgery; he could work conscientiously, but never put his heart into it. He had been born and bred in the country; like old Douglas he "loved better to hear the lark sing, than the mouse squeak"; and yet he had voluntarily accepted such a life as this.

But then came second thoughts. He recalled his feeling of despair when the knowledge of his altered fortunes had come to him first. How grateful he had felt to old Cottrell for opening a door into the realm of toil and independence!

It was better to fag away at an uncongenial task than to stay at home, eating the bread of idleness, and using up the small portion set aside for his mother and the girls. They would never have told him to go,—those good people at the old house;—they would never, by look or by word have reproached him for staying. But his own manly spirit had told him the right thing to do; and he would do it at any cost.

Sometimes when people go forth into the wilderness to seek their bread, they find honey to make it sweet. Sometimes when the path of duty leads across a waste, the strange land blooms with unexpected flowers. Coming up to town to do old Cottrell's bidding, Mayne had found one blossom rich enough to brighten a desert. Nelly was in London; the very thought of her was as a glimpse of paradise.

Not far away, that same morning, a conversation was going on which would have interested young Comberford.

The scene was a room upstairs in one of the largest houses in Russell Square. Lady Florence Camden, a woman of seven and forty, well preserved, and of an aristocratic type, leant back in an easy-chair, lazily looking over some letters. Nelly Stanley, standing near the toilet-table, in an unembarrassed attitude, had just answered her question.

"If Louie had not spoken I should have told

you everything, as I always do, Lady Florence,"
said the girl, in her musical voice. "When
Mr. Comberford wrote to say that he wanted
to see me, I let him know that I was going
to the chapel on Sunday morning."

"But why couldn't he have called here,
child?" her ladyship demanded. "What was
the good of a mysterious assignation with a
man you had never seen?"

"It was because I had never seen him that
I made the assignation." Nelly smiled, and
flushed slightly. "I did not know whether he
would be presentable. As he was poor dear
Angela's brother I rather expected him to be
of the bumpkin type. And yet I wished to see
him for her sake."

"There is nothing of the bumpkin about him
if one can believe Louie's description. That
little monkey is getting too precocious," Lady
Florence remarked.

"A great deal too precocious," Nelly assented.

"But she is right about Mr. Comberford. He is a gentleman."

"Good-looking, I suppose!"

"Yes."

"And he is coming to live in London?"

"Yes. He will act as secretary to his god-father, a Mr. Cottrell."

"Do you mean Sylvester Cottrell, the man who writes books on magic?"

"Yes," answered Nelly again.

"Let me see," said Lady Florence, lifting her blue eyes to the governess, and surveying her with a thoughtful air. "There were some Comber-fords at a place in Sussex. My brother Percy used to go there for the shooting sometimes. Are they your Comberfords, I wonder?"

"Perhaps they are. Angela's people have lived at Hartside for generations."

"Hartside; yes. Percy was quite enthusiastic about the scenery, and he liked the old house. Of course Mr. Comberford will want to see you again for his sister's sake." Lady Florence smiled demurely. "Let him come, and give him tea in the orthodox way. And do look after Louie, and snub her now and then. If you find her quite irrepressible send her to me."

She returned to her letters; and Nelly, with a slower step than usual, went down to the schoolroom. The lecture from Lady Florence, which she had expected and was prepared for, had passed off pleasantly enough. Nothing had been said to irritate the governess, who was well known to be a favourite with the most important member of the household. And yet any one who had seen the soft glow which overspread Nelly's face would have thought that she was strangely agitated.

But it was not of Lady Florence that the girl was thinking as she went down the wide staircase.

CHAPTER III.

THE SECOND MEETING.

She walks in beauty, like the night
Of cloudless climes and starry skies.
BYRON.

As Nelly had said, the Camdens were a legal race; Lady Camden, the nominal mistress of the house in Russell Square, was the widow of a well-known judge. Giffard, her eldest son and a successful barrister, had married Lady Florence Layter, daughter of the Earl of Etherleigh. Percy, the second son, was a judge in India; and, having lost his wife, had sent his two children home to his mother. It was Lady Florence who looked after the little ones and engaged their governess; and in short every one who knew the Camdens could see at a glance that it was Lady Florence who governed the whole family.

How did she do it? She had a quiet, half-lazy manner which gave people the idea that she was a woman of no resolution at all. She did not look as if she could domineer over anybody; her tall, slender figure was as flexible as ribbon-grass; her face was a long oval, delicately-featured; her eyes were so long and so narrow that you only saw a line of bright blue when you met their gaze. Her dark-brown hair was still plentiful, and but slightly grey; she made no effort to appear younger than she really was, but you felt instinctively that she would grow old slowly, and with a grace peculiar to herself.

No one wondered that the handsome barrister had married a woman who was seven years older than himself. Lady Florence had willed that he should fall in love with her, and he did.

She had never been a beauty; but she had

always possessed the indescribable power of swaying the hearts and influencing the minds around her. Giffard Camden never knew that she had drawn him to her with invisible threads that were stronger than steel; he firmly believed that he had fallen in love with her of his own accord. They had been married eight years, and her influence still dominated his life; her grace and refinement charmed him still.

When a new governess was wanted for Percy's children, Lady Florence went to a well-known ladies' college and consulted the principal. Nelly Stanley was warmly recommended; and Lady Florence was glad to secure a bright girl, fresh from the school-room. Moreover Nelly's beauty pleased her, and Nelly's friendlessness excited her compassion.

The children took kindly to Miss Stanley at once. She was clever, and had a way of making lessons agreeable. Giffard Camden congratulated his wife on having selected such a pleasant and capable young person. But Miss Camden, the maiden aunt who lived in Woburn Square, suggested that it was dangerous to have such a pretty girl in the house.

"What mischief will she do?" inquired Lady Florence languidly.

"Well, my dear, it is difficult to say;" Miss Camden replied. "But she is so *very* pretty, you know."

"I do know it, and I am glad of it, Aunt Margery. If we want to keep young, we must surround ourselves with youth and beauty. Do you wish me to be like Rachel Esmond? I have always thought her one of the most detestable creatures in fiction. Don't you remember the ugly set of servants at Castlewood? The housekeeper was old; my lady's own waiting-woman squinted, and was marked with small-pox. It has sometimes seemed to me that Rachel courted all her misfortunes."

Miss Camden shook her head and declared

that it was quite impossible to argue with Florence. But as time went on, and no harm came of Nelly's presence in the house, the anxious spinster became accustomed to her beauty, and even vouchsafed her a smile now and then.

A year had glided peacefully away in Russell Square, and Miss Stanley had not troubled the Camdens with any romantic adventures. Mrs. Camden approved of her in a cold and stately fashion; Lady Florence treated her with frank goodwill; Louie liked her, and Robby adored her. No young governess ever had easier duties or a happier home. Nelly was by no means ungrateful for all the good things that fell to her lot; she had a healthy appetite and slept soundly at nights; and yet she was distinctly conscious that life must have something better in store for her than this. She wanted something to happen; she was tired of unbroken peace; but she had never candidly confessed to herself that she was expecting a lover. Still, she was sure that he could not be very long in coming;

> "Somewhere or other, may be far or near,
> With just a wall, a hedge between,"

he was waiting for the moment which should bring him to the queen of his heart.

There were those who could have told her that sometimes the wall never crumbles away, and the hedge is never broken through. Two hearts, who might have met and mingled, may wait through a life-time with the barrier between them; and each is bitterly conscious of all that might have been.

Lady Florence was the only person in the household who suspected Nelly of mental restlessness. She knew that the girl was waiting for her "hereafter," and smiled to herself.

No one knew better than Lady Florence that the "hereafter," when we come to it, bears only a fleeting resemblance to the golden land which we have seen in our dreams. She had trained herself through long years of self-study, and could have told precisely the day and hour at which she had won the victory over early emotions. But she still felt a good-natured pity for one whose feet were on the borders of the Enchanted Ground.

She watched Nelly closely, and saw certain signs that foretold the beginning of a romance. The note to young Comberford was written and despatched; and on a Thursday afternoon he presented himself in Russell Square.

He found Nelly in a pretty little apartment known as the breakfast-room, although break-fast was very seldom taken there. After he had talked to her for ten minutes, Lady Florence glided in, and soon discovered that he belonged sufficiently to her world to make it pleasant to chat with him. She liked the young man at once. He was tall and well set up, and had a clear-cut English face with deep blue eyes that were beautiful. Of course she saw that he

had fallen under the spell of Nelly's beauty;
and having made his acquaintance she glided
away, as softly as she had come; and he was
alone with his divinity.

Nelly was very bright and unaffected. There
were real tears in her eyes when he gave her a
little pearl locket which had belonged to Angela.

"She wished you to have it," he said.

"I have seen her wear it a hundred times.
It reminds me of the dear old days," she
answered. "If I had only known that I should
never meet her again, I should have asked her
many questions! Our last hours were wasted
in school-girls' talk. I wish I could have them
over again."

"That's a very old wish, I fancy," Mayne
said thoughtfully. "But if you could have those
hours over again I don't think you would say
anything of great importance. You were both
so young, you know, and your lives had been
so uneventful. I can imagine that a chief,

whose moments were numbered, would have
many things to say to his right-hand man.   But
Angela, dear child, what could she have said?"

"She would have told me to make friends of
those whom she had loved."

"And she told us to remember you."   His
blue eyes were fixed on hers.   "She knew that
we should keep our promise and find you out.
Now that we have found you, Miss Stanley,
we shall not lose you.   You must come to
Hartside before this summer is over."

Nelly compressed her pretty lips with a
doubtful air.

"I should like to come," she said.   "But I'm
afraid that I cannot be spared.   Lady Florence
will want me to spend my holidays with the
children."

"But you are always with the children!   They
must give you a little time to devote to your
friends," cried Mayne, with rising indignation.

"But I am supposed to have no friends,"

replied Nelly quietly. "When Lady Florence engaged me she was told that I was quite alone in the world. And so of course it was arranged that I should stay with the Camdens always."

"There must be a change," Mayne said in a decided tone.

"Must there? I had almost begun to think that life had no changes in store for me, or only the inevitable change from youth to age. I dare say I shall see my hair getting grey, and crows feet coming at the corners of my eyes," added Nelly composedly, "but I don't expect any other breaks in my monotonous career."

"It is very early to have done with expectation," said the young fellow, smiling.

She gave him some tea, and looked at him for a moment with inquiring eyes. The room was quiet; there were roses on the table; she had a scarlet geranium in her bodice; long afterwards he could recall every trivial detail of that time. He could remember the soft fawn-coloured dress that she wore, and even the touches of gold in her deep-brown hair when the light shone upon it. Out of doors there was a glimpse of a London garden where flowers were few and leaves many. A plaster nymph in one corner of the ground was decorated with an old straw hat of Robby's, and seemed to be enjoying herself in a rakish fashion; and Robby was digging vigorously in a little piece of earth, under a plane-tree, while the nymph watched him with her head on one side. Louie, in a dainty frock and sun-bonnet, paced slowly up and down a gravelled walk, giving a stealthy glance now and then at the window of the breakfast-room.

"All the best time of your life is to come," said Mayne, answering the question in the beautiful eyes. "You will attract happiness as naturally as the flower attracts the bee. Every-thing that is bright and loving will fly to your sweetness. You are one of the favoured few who are destined to enjoy life."

"Are you a fortune-teller?" demanded Nelly, with a little smile of incredulity.

"Your fortune is written in your face," he responded gallantly.

"Hundreds of girls could tell you that pretty faces don't make pretty fortunes," she answered with a sigh. "Perhaps my mother was beautiful."

"Do you remember her?" he asked with quick interest.

"No." Nelly's dark lashes veiled her brown eyes for a moment. "I sometimes wonder whether it would have been well or ill for me to have known her? When the girls at school talked about their mothers, I used to try to fancy what my life would have been if I had not lost mine?"

There was something simple and tender in her tone that went to Mayne's heart. His eyes met hers, and she could read his thoughts in them.

"Don't pity me, Mr. Comberford," she said suddenly. "I always feel soft and silly when any one is sorry for me. When people are cold and matter-of-fact they make me quite brave. I thrive best in a sharp, bracing atmosphere, I suppose. I will not talk to you about myself again."

"Talk of nothing else!" he exclaimed, and the words sprang to his lips before he could check them. "I want to hear a great deal more,—I am hungering for more." She looked at him thoughtfully with a grave face.

"Ah, you are kind," she said after a pause. "But I must not test your kindness too severely."

CHAPTER IV.

LOVERS.

"Now therefore I do rest
A prophet certain of my prophecy,
That never shadow of mistrust can cross
Between us." TENNYSON.

Two young faces were to be seen under the trees of Lincoln's Inn on a Sunday afternoon, when the summer was three weeks older. They had met by appointment in the spot which they had both learnt to regard as their natural trysting-place. In past days Nelly had noted all the charms of this sequestered nook, but with a dispassionate admiration. Now the long, shady walk was touched with the sunlight of Paradise, and the lazy coo of the pigeons was as sweet as an old love-song learnt in childhood and recalled in womanhood. The prince, long waited for, had come to the princess, and the everyday prose of life had changed into a fairy tale.

Louie and Robby had been carried off, after morning service, by Aunt Margery; and were spending the day in Woburn Square. No one had asked any questions when the governess had put on her bonnet and gone out with a large prayer-book in her hand. The prayer-book had red-edged leaves and could be seen by any one who happened to look out of the windows.

Nelly's face was composed and good,—so composed and good that Lady Florence smiled at the sight of her.

"She isn't going to church any more than I am," thought her ladyship, sinking back on the cushions of her luxurious chair. "I am not deceived by the outward and visible signs of piety. That was how I used to look when I went out to meet Charlie Temple in the old days. Dear me, what summers we had then!"

She mused, with her head a little on one side, and her long white fingers beating a gentle tattoo upon the arm of the chair.

" I suppose those two young noodles will be very happy together," she went on. "We may laugh at our first love, but it is a delicious thing, after all;—the choicest morsel in the banquet of life. Good solid food may be spread for us afterwards; but there is nothing like the ambrosial sweetness of that first love feast. These warm afternoons are making me senti-mental; I had quite a clear vision of Charlie's face just then. How curiously distinct a memory-picture is! I saw him just as plainly as if he were here beside my chair, instead of lying in his lonely African grave. Well, well, supposing we had had our dream out, and run away together, shouldn't we have got fearfully tired of each other long ago?"

So Lady Florence drifted back to the days of her youth; and Mayne and Nelly passed

on side by side into the Eden which her ladyship had known and lost.

The pigeons cooed; the warm lights and
delicate shadows lay all around them on the walk;
the sleepy quietness of the old Inn garden was
unbroken by any harsher sounds than bird or leaf
could make. Nelly sat silently in her corner of
the bench, trying to realize the bliss of this
sunshiny moment before it took wing; and Mayne
watched her, feasting his eyes upon her face as
if he could never have enough of her beauty.

"Nelly," he said, in a hushed voice, "will
you not let me take care of you for the future?
I want you, darling, for my very own. Will
you not promise yourself to me? There may
be some time to wait, and then a quiet life and
a humble home; but you will never know a
deeper love than mine. No work will seem
wearisome when I am working for you. A
man can do wonderful things, dear, for the sake
of the woman who is the queen of his heart.

You are my queen, Nelly; come and take your throne."

He had moved a little closer to her as he spoke, and his hand sought hers, and imprisoned it in a firm clasp.

Nelly drew a long breath, and then turned towards him with a swift movement, her beautiful face alight with feeling.

"Are you sure that you know me well enough to want me?" she asked tremulously. "I am so poor—so lonely—I cannot even be certain that I have a right to my name. Let me tell all that I can tell about my poor little self before I answer you."

"Answer me first, dear, and tell me your story afterwards."

"But, Mr. Comberford, you must listen—"

"I can't listen to anything till you have told me that you love me."

"Isn't it too soon to tell you? We met only three weeks ago for the first time."

"My darling, love has nothing to do with

time. We met three centuries ago at least, and I have always adored you. No true love is ever new; it is sweet, and familiar, and old as the hills."

The custodians of Lincoln's Inn are sober men, well stricken in years, and accustomed to take their rightful share of repose on Sunday afternoons. They have been young themselves, and are far too well-bred to think of prowling round a spot that lovers have made their own. Not one of these respectable persons would have forgotten himself so far as to walk in the direction of that shady path where our couple were sitting under the trees.

So there was no looker-on to see that Nelly permitted herself to be drawn into Mayne's arms. The pigeons droned on, cooing all her scruples away, and lulling her heart to rest. He kissed her; and the first touch of those velvet lips was printed on his life.

"But now," she said, after a brief silence,

"you must hear this miserable little story of mine. And if, after hearing it, you change your mind, I will promise not to blame you."

He smiled with superb scorn. "Do you think a man's mind changes so easily?" he asked.

"We will see," she answered demurely. "Are you going to hold my hand all the while? Hadn't we better sit farther apart?"

"Nonsense," he rejoined promptly, coming closer. "No one can see us excepting through a strong glass. Besides, the whole place is asleep on Sundays. You don't mind the pigeons, do you? Nelly, what a wonderful colour your hair is, rich brown, with dashes of gold in it, and it grows in little ripples and twists."

"I know all about it," said Nelly frankly, "and I suspect it's very rough at this moment. Will you be quiet, please, and let me tell my story?"

Mayne settled himself in a comfortable listening attitude, with her hand in his.

"The first place I can remember is an

old-fashioned house at Hornsey," she began.
"It was a school for very little children; but
none of the pupils were so small as I was
when they took me there. As I grew older I
began to look forward to the visits of a lady
who always brought me presents. She was not
my mother, they said; but Mrs. Merriwell,—
the best friend I had in the world."

"The lady who adopted you? I have heard
Angela speak of her," interrupted Mayne, as
a flash of remembrance crossed his mind.

"Angela once spent a Sunday in Harley
Street with Mrs. Merriwell and me," Nelly
replied. "I was allowed to invite my friend.
But of course that was a long time after I had
left Hornsey. I did not go to the college till
I was thirteen; and I was quite a big girl when
Mrs. Merriwell first told me how she found me."

She paused, and a cloud passed over the
brightness of her face. The roses on her cheeks
paled a little; the lips quivered.

"This is the part that I hate telling," she said, with a sigh. "I'll get over it as quickly as I can."

Mayne's fingers closed firmly on the little hand he held. The warm clasp gave her courage to go on.

"Mrs. Merriwell was left a widow when she was very young," Nelly continued. "She was rich, and had few relations to interfere with her, so that she did exactly as she liked. She was fond of the country, and always took a house in some unfrequented spot when the summer came. One summer she found a place in a wild part of Hampshire where there are acres of bracken and heather, and lovely woods of oak and beech. It is called Heatherbeck. Do you know it?"

"I went there when I was a boy," Mayne answered. "It is a beautiful place."

"She was driving one evening along a lonely road when she caught sight of something by the wayside. It was a child, about two years old, sitting on the ground, and pulling at the grass and wild flowers. There it sat, babbling and murmuring to itself, as happy as a princess. It was a merry little thing, with a curly brown head and brown eyes."

"Dear Nelly, that child was you!"

"Yes; the carriage was moving slowly uphill, and Mrs. Merriwell had time to notice me. It seems that I was not a shy child. I laughed, and pointed at the lady with my finger; and she fell in love with me at once."

"Quite natural," said Mayne.

"That laugh of mine decided my fate. If I had chanced to be shy I should have cried and looked hideous, and then I suppose I should have been left sitting on the grass. Mrs. Merriwell was an impulsive woman; she stopped the carriage, got out, and took me up in her arms."

The girl paused once more, and drew her

breath quickly. Her lover would have drawn her towards him, but she held back.

"No, Mayne, don't be too tender," she entreated. "Don't even let me think that you are pitying me in your heart. It will take the strength out of me, and I hate to show weakness. Let me go on."

"Why not tell me the rest another time, darling," he asked.

"I want to get it over," she repeated impatiently. "Well, Mrs. Merriwell kissed and fondled me until she wanted to have me for her own. Her companion, a Miss Winter, suggested that my people could not be far off, and that it would be wise to put me back on the grass. But Mrs. Merriwell would not listen to wisdom. After looking round in search of my relations, and finding no one, she resolved to take me home with her. As I have said, I was a brown baby, and close to the spot where I was found there were traces of a gipsy encampment. So they decided that I must be a gipsy."

"And then?" said Mayne.

"There is really nothing more to tell. I was clean, and my clothing was neat, although plain and poor. There was no clue to my belongings; the spot was watched by a rural policeman, but no one ever came there to look for me. The gipsies who had camped there were said to be Stanleys, and there is little doubt that I belonged to them. Mrs. Merriwell took entire possession of me from that hour. She had me baptized, giving me the name of Nelly, because it had been the name of a dead sister of her own. And I have always been known as Nelly Stanley."

"But it is by no means certain that you are a Stanley," Mayne remarked.

"Mrs. Merriwell believed that I was. As a baby I was much browner than I am now; and I had a gay red-and-yellow handkerchief, such as gipsies wear, tied over my shoulders. As I grew older I betrayed a strong taste for bright colours, and you see I love a bit of scarlet to this day! Yes; I think you must make up your mind to accept me as a gipsy."

There was a brief silence. Then she looked up into her lover's face half wistfully, yet with a gleam of mirth in her beautiful eyes.

"Mayne," she said, "are you quite sure that you want me still?"

"Surer than ever, my darling. And if any one happens to have a strong glass he may look through it to his heart's content;—I'm going to kiss you again. Oh Nelly, what a sweet thing you are! Nothing on earth—no cloud, no shadow—shall ever come between you and me!"

CHAPTER V.

Thine eyes are stars of morning,
Thy lips are crimson flowers.

LONGFELLOW.

"So you want to go and stay with your new friends at Hartside," said Lady Florence.

"Yes, please;" Nelly answered. "But they don't feel like new friends."

"I suppose not," Lady Florence rejoined. "There is a sweet sense of familiarity, and all that sort of thing. Well, my dear, you have been a good girl, and you deserve a holiday. Only I don't know how we shall tell Robby that he will not see you for a whole month. That boy is the loudest roarer I have ever known."

"He's a dear, good little man," said the

young governess with real feeling. " I wish I
could take him with me to Hartside!"

"Oh, you will find it quite possible to exist
without Robby! I think I must send the children
to the seaside," added Lady Florence, after a
moment's reflection. "Aunt Margery will be glad
to have them with her at Eastbourne. Of course
they will wear her out and shatter her nerves,
but that can't be helped; and she will feel that
I am showing confidence in her by intrusting
them to her care. I am afraid I cannot give
you more than a month, Miss Stanley."

"Thank you," said Nelly gratefully. "A
month is quite as long a time as I can expect
to have."

"That's how you feel now," remarked Lady
Florence, with a twinkle of fun in her eyes.
"Three weeks hence you will be complaining
piteously of my tyrannical conditions. As to
Mr. Comberford, I dare say he already thinks
of me as an ogress."

"Indeed, Lady Florence, he thinks you have been very gracious to him." Nelly's voice was very sweet in its earnestness. "And he knows how good you have been to me."

"So you have been talking to him about yourself, child? How soon you two have got upon confidential terms! Of course your school friendship with the sister paved the way to intimacy with the brother; it is all very pretty and natural and romantic. Does he know the very beginning of your little life-story, so far as you know it yourself?"

"I have told him everything that Mrs. Merriwell told me," answered Nelly frankly.

"Ah, yes. And he was interested, no doubt. The Comberfords are an old family, I believe," said Lady Florence in a musing tone.

"I suppose so. I don't know much about pedigrees, I'm afraid," Nelly replied meekly. "It would have been much nicer for me if Mrs. Merriwell had found out a little more about my poor mother," she added after a pause.

"It might not have been nicer for you, my dear." Lady Florence looked at her kindly. "Sometimes we may be thankful for the mysteries that are never cleared up. It was certainly a pity that Mrs. Merriwell didn't live longer; you might have had a happy home with her for years. To die before you left school, and leave you only five hundred pounds! It was really sad."

"Yes, it was sad," said Nelly. "And it would have been sadder still if I had loved her better."

"You did not love her?" Lady Florence exclaimed.

"Not as much as I ought. She only took a fancy to me, you see; she didn't really love me. And she never felt any interest in my poor mother's history; if she had cared for me very much she would have found out how I came to be sitting all alone by the roadside."

Nelly's voice was trembling; her dark eyes

had a far-away look in them; Lady Florence had never seen her so much moved before.

"My dear child," she said gently, "we mustn't look too closely into the motives of those who are kind to us. Take the kindness, and be duly grateful for it; never inquire whether it came from the depths of the heart or only from the surface."

"Some hearts have no depths," murmured Nelly.

"So much the better for them, perhaps," said Lady Florence with a slight movement of her graceful shoulders. "Don't go in for philosophy and analysis and all those dangerous things, child; they take the sweetness out of life, and life is by no means over-filled with sweetness. Enjoy yourself at Hartside; make the most of your beauty and brightness; freely you have received, freely give. I dare say they will all learn to love you so much that it will be a hard matter to get you back."

"Oh, they will understand that I am only lent for a month," replied Nelly, brightening at the thought of her holiday. She had been silent about her engagement; partly because the joy was so new that she wanted to keep it all to herself for the present; and partly because she had a natural subtlety in guarding a secret. Even at school she had never cared to tell everything as most of the girls did. Excepting Angela, not one of her companions had ever known that she had been picked up by the roadside. They had been informed that she was Mrs. Merriwell's adopted child, and that was all.

The day of her departure came soon. Robby's roaring shook the house to its very foundations; and Lady Florence shut herself up in her bedroom and stopped her ears. Even Louie wept in a subdued fashion; but Miss Camden, who witnessed the leave-taking, was much displeased by this display of regret. It was silly, she remarked, for little girls and boys to make such

a fuss about saying good-bye to their governess
when they had a kind grand-aunt to take care
of them.   Besides, Miss Stanley was only going
away for four short weeks.

"B—b--but s'pose she should be st—st
—stole!" sobbed the agonized Robby.

"Nonsense, Robby, no one wants to steal
her," said Aunt Margery severely.   "You are
a naughty boy to stammer so dreadfully."

"I sh—sh—shall st—st—stammer till she
c—c—comes back," declared Robby, getting
crimson with temper.   "J--j—just see if I
don't!"

Miss Camden was exasperated to such a
degree that she threatened to whip him; and
it was, perhaps, well for all parties that Lady
Florence, having heard Nelly's cab roll away,
came downstairs again at that moment.

"I am sorry that you should be provoked,
dear aunt," she said, with her never-failing
courtesy.   "But Robby will be good without

whipping. His uncle says he is to have a splendid bucket and spade to take down to the seaside, and nurse will go out with him to buy them. Now, Robby, be a man, and don't go out of doors with a baby's crying face."

This appeal to his manhood was not without effect on the little lord of creation. He conquered himself with an effort, and was led peacefully away.

"I'm afraid it will be rather difficult to get on without Miss Stanley," Lady Florence said confidentially to her husband. "I foresee that Aunt Margery and Robby the Roarer will come to blows."

"Then I hope that Robby the Roarer will get the best of it," replied Giffard Camden heartily. "It's hard on the little man to have Aunt Margery forced upon him instead of his pretty Stanley girl. He adores his governess, and he's very good when she's with him. Why do those Comberford people want to take her away?"

"It's the Comberford young man who wants to take her away. Robby suggests—'s'pose she should be st—st—stole?' I am afraid that his fears are not altogether groundless," said Lady Florence.

"Oh, you think young Comberford is smitten? Well, it isn't surprising, and I think the girl has behaved very well. She might have had a train of danglers if she had wanted them. But she has a good deal of common sense."

"Yes, she has common sense," assented Lady Florence thoughtfully. "But that is a quality which sometimes deserts a woman when she needs it most."

The woody slopes all round the quiet station were bathed in sunshine when Nelly arrived at Hartside. It was about four o'clock in the afternoon, and the warm golden light of early August lay on road and hill; here and there a silver ribbon of water gleamed out of the shadows; the grey spire of a church tapered up into the clear air; the walls of the vicarage, close by, were half hidden under a foam of clematis. Mayne Comberford was standing on the platform, watching the train with anxious eyes as it came gliding into the station; and near him stood the vicar with his eldest daughter.

It was hard on the young fellow that these two excellent persons should chance to witness his meeting with his betrothed. But who does not know how inopportunely our friends often cross our path? They bear down upon us, smiling and self-important, when our sweetheart waits only a little way off. Or they meet us with outstretched hands and beaming eyes in some spot where we had fondly deemed ourselves secure from observation. It is, on the whole, a surprising thing that humanity endures these continual exasperations with such admirable self-control.

Mayne's patience very nearly broke down under the strain put upon it that day. Mr.

Payton, a worthy man who had known Mayne Comberford in knickerbockers, began to suspect his young friend of a guilty conscience; but Miss Christina, with the keen insight of her sex, attributed the poor fellow's reserve and shyness to the true cause. She had not, however, the generosity to lead her father away. If Mayne was expecting somebody to arrive by the train, she was firmly resolved to see who that somebody was. Of course it was a woman; but what sort of woman? The vicarage generally made itself acquainted with all that was happening, or likely to happen, at the manor. But the Comberford girls had been invisible for a few days; and when Miss Payton had called, Mrs. Comberford had not said one word about an expected guest.

The train came slowly into the station; and without even saying "excuse me" Mayne left Christina in the middle of a sentence, and rushed wildly to the door of a second-class carriage. Another moment, and such a vision of beauty descended on the platform that the vicar and his daughter stared in dumb amazement.

Nelly, dressed as carefully and tastefully as usual, was looking as fresh as if she had just stepped from her own room, instead of out of the dusty compartment. She wore a black lace hat of singular gracefulness, laden with a bunch of poppies, and a little handkerchief of scarlet silk peeped out of the bodice of her grey gown. Her face, with its brilliant depth of complexion, was glowing under the shady hat with the richness of a tropical flower. There was the piquancy of merry mischief in that exquisite face; it is quite possible that Nelly saw, as in a lightning flash, the effect she had produced on the Paytons, and secretly enjoyed the sensation she had made. "Darling," Mayne whispered, "I hate to feel that those two wooden-headed creatures are looking at you."

But Nelly did not hate the feeling at all;

she had a nutural pleasure in being looked at.

"It doesn't hurt me," she said.

"There's a fly waiting outside," Mayne continued. "Is there only one box dear? How moderate you are! That hat is the most perfect thing I've seen for a long time; we shall have all Hartside copying it."

"Give my love to the girls, and say that I shall see them to-morrow," cried Christina as the pair swept past her. Mayne was visibly agitated; Nelly was as cool and stately as a young queen.

The musty old fly received the lovers on its capacious seat; the driver whipped up his heavy horse; and the lumbering conveyance rolled ponderously along a lovely road, tree-shaded, and sweet with the rich breath of honey-suckle. Nelly enjoyed the fragrance and fresh-ness with a child's delight; it seemed to her, just then, that she had been born to live in a world of sunny lights and leafy glooms like these around her.

"Look," she said suddenly, "there's a gipsy encampment. See that brown baby rolling on the grass. Mayne, I was like that once."

"Don't, dear," he answered, with a pained look. "Forget all about that far-away past. Let us banish it for ever."

CHAPTER VI.

INTRODUCED TO THE FAMILY.

But Heaven in thy creation did decree
That in thy face sweet love should ever dwell;
Whate'er thy thoughts on thy heart's working be,
Thy looks should nothing thence but sweetness tell.
  How like Eve's apple doth thy beauty grow,
  If thy sweet virtue answer not thy show.
                                SHAKSPEARE.

NELLY gave her lover one of those swift glances
which seem to pierce a man through and through:
but he did not meet her eyes at that moment.
She had seen that he had winced at her chance
allusion to her gipsy babyhood, and her heart
darkened, but she made no sign.

He had listened to her story under the trees
of Lincoln's Inn, and had loved her the better
after she had told it. But here, among his own
woods and fields, he was another man, she said

to herself; the influences of family associations and family pride were as strong, or stronger, than her own. She held her head high, as this thought came into her mind; but she kept silence. As a child it had been remarked of her that she had a wonderful gift for holding her tongue; and Mayne did not even dream that she had resented his words.

But she *had* resented them. They had hinted that there was something about her that he was ashamed of, and wanted to forget; and she had believed that she had come to Hartside to be worshipped as a queen.

The fly rumbled slowly up the slope of a woody lane; and then the old manor house came suddenly into view. It was a warm red house, with many gables, set deep in rich foliage, and wreathed with creepers and roses from garret to basement:—an English home, hallowed by family love, and dignified by the upright lives of the good old race of Comberfords. And

as you passed between the stone gateposts, and
heard the cawing of the rooks from the pine
wood, you felt that you had left the feverish
world behind, and entered into an atmosphere
of peace and rest.

A well-kept lawn, darkened by the shadow of
a grand old cedar, lay in front of the house;
scarlet and yellow flower-beds made brilliant
spots of colour on the green; a couple of cane
chairs, and a little rustic table, laden with
books and a work-basket, told that the ladies
of the household had been spending the afternoon out of doors. Nelly, sitting in stately
ease by her lover's side, was watching keenly
for the first flutter of summer dresses in the
porch. But not the vestige of a gown was to
be seen; and she fought a quick, fierce little
battle with pride and dismay.

The arrival at Hartside was not in the least
like the scene she had pictured in her mind.
Nelly was a girl in her teens, conscious of her

own striking beauty, and exulting in her con quest. It was not unnatural that she should have expected to be welcomed with a flourish of trumpets. Mayne was so very much in love, and his people were so devoted to him, that she had been quite prepared to be rapturously received by the whole family.

Mayne himself was looking out anxiously for some of the members of the household. He had not thought that his mother would come out to welcome his betrothed with effusion ; but he had hoped that Susie or Phyllis would have been standing in the porch ; or that little Madge and Rosa would have run down the drive to meet the carriage at the gate. A chill crept over him as they drew near the house ; and Nelly, with her keen instinct, felt that he was ill at ease.

"I wonder where they all are !" he said, trying to speak lightly. "Out in the garden, I suppose. But they'll hear the wheels in a minute."

The driver stopped before the great portico,
now covered with masses of climbing roses;
and Nelly, looking through the open door, saw
a tall girlish figure in the hall.   She stepped
gracefully out of the old fly, just touching her
lover's arm as she alighted, and he was positively
grateful to her for her perfect self-possession.
Of course he was feeling a little worried, he
said to himself; but Nelly, poor darling, did
not know that the mother had been a trifle
upset by the news of the engagement, and she
was as unembarrassed as a child.

Little did he suspect that his lady-love had
divined everything, although she had been told
nothing!   It is seldom indeed that a young
man fully realizes the marvellous acuteness of
a young woman.

Susie Comberford came forward to greet the
new-comer with a heart full of good intentions.
She dearly loved her brother, and honestly wanted
him to be happy in his own way.   But Nelly's grace

and beauty absolutely bewildered and dazzled her.

She had listened good-humouredly to Mayne's account of the perfections of his betrothed, and had said, half laughing and half sighing, that he was following in Angela's footprints. And she had been fully prepared to see a pretty girl, just a year older than herself, fresh and frank and simple, with the atmosphere of the school-room around her still. But this lovely belle, with her calm manner, and air of distinction, was an overwhelming surprise.

"How do you do," she said, shaking hands, and quite forgetting that she had meant to give her future sister-in-law a kiss. "I hope you are not very tired after your journey?"

"Oh no," responded Nelly composedly. "I am not easily tired."

Mayne thought that his sister was intentionally cold and stiff, and glared at her with angry disapproval. Susie, embarrassed by the glare, became colder and stiffer.

"This is my sister Phyllis," she said, as another tall girl appeared, and offered her hand. "Will you come into the drawing-room and see mother?"

Nelly, in her soft grey dress, glided easily into the pleasant, oak-panelled room which Angela and Mayne had already described to her. It was warm with afternoon sunshine, and sweet with the breath of many flowers; but Nelly did not feel that she had come into a genial atmosphere. Mrs. Comberford was kind; she was more cordial than her daughters had been, and did not forget to give the orthodox kiss; yet the kindness and the kiss seemed flat and tame to the girl who had expected so much.

She followed Susie to her room with a chilly sense of disappointment which no one suspected. The staircase was easy and broad; there was an open gallery running round the hall; and Susie unclosed one of the doors with an air of quiet primness.

"You will easily find your way down to us,"
she said. "I am sure you must want a cup
of tea."

They had given her a pretty room, Nelly
thought; everything was of an antique grace
which recalled the maidens of a past generation. Girls in short-waisted gowns had decked
themselves before the toilet-glass in the oval
frame, and made themselves beautiful in the
fashion of long ago. Out of doors there was
a world of woods and low hills, sweet and
silent and splendid in the sunshine. A scent
of jessamine was everywhere; thousands of white
flower-stars looked in at the opened windows.
Nelly took off the black lace hat, and pressed
the little curls of dark brown hair into order.
She bathed her face, and went downstairs fresh
and glowing as a rose.

Mr. Comberford had come indoors, and was
standing on the hearth-rug, with his back to
the empty grate, when Nelly returned to the

drawing-room. Mayne, who watched his father closely, saw that he was struck, and almost startled by her beauty.

"I am glad to welcome you to Hartside," said Mr. Comberford, with an old-fashioned stateliness which sat very well upon him. "You come in the time of flowers and sunshine,—the time that suits you best." Something in his tone and manner revived Nelly's drooping spirits. Here was the most important member of the household showing that he, at any rate, was not quite blind to her attractions.

"I love sunshine," she said, looking up into his face with her sweet sunny smile.

"You are made to bask in it," he answered, retaining the little hand that he held, and leading her to a seat near the open window. Then he brought a little cane table to her side; Susie supplied her with tea, and Mayne came up with cake and bread-and-butter. All were kind; all were courteous; but Nelly thought she could detect a shade on Mrs. Comberford's brow.

"Mayne's mother has set herself against me," she mused. "I think she means to sit upon me. Well, let her try, that's all."

And Nelly's smile was at its sweetest when she looked in the direction of the comely matron who sat near the tea-tray. Recalling Lady Florence's unfailing tact and graceful self-possession she felt herself perfectly able to cope with these good country people who had lived in such a narrow world of their own.

But if their world was narrow it was lovely. After tea, Mayne led his betrothed out of doors, and showed her his favourite walk at the back of the house. It was a path through a wood rising gently up the side of one of those low hills which encompassed the village. The ascent was too gradual to tire the weariest feet, and Nelly was not weary. She was glad to be in the open air, alone with her lover once more.

"Oh, Mayne, how sweet it is here!" she cried, standing still and looking up at the blue sky through a lattice of boughs and leaves.

"You would enjoy a country life, Nelly." His face came between hers and the sky. "I wish I had money enough to rent Rosedown,—a charming place about three miles away, belonging to Lord Rexbury. But I shall have to work hard to make a home for you in London, dear; and we will spend our summer holidays here always. My mother and the girls will soon be devoted to you."

"Will they?" Nelly asked a little doubt-fully.

"Of course they will. Susie and Phyllis are shy; they haven't poor Angela's easy manner. And my mother seems grave until she is well known; but she is very nice, isn't she?"

"Very nice," Nelly answered blandly. "And your father is perfectly delightful."

"You made a conquest of him at once,"

Mayne said, with a satisfied smile. "Let me see, this is Friday, isn't it?"

"Yes, it is Friday; an unlucky day for my first coming to the manor." Nelly started as she spoke. "Why are you thinking about the day, Mayne?"

"My dearest child, is it possible that you are superstitious? I am thinking that we are close upon Sunday, that's all. On August Sundays our little church is often patronized by a good many smart people, and I was wondering how many heads you will turn."

"Who are the smart people, Mayne?" asked Nelly, forgetting her momentary thrill of uneasiness.

"Well, there's Lord Rexbury's household, to begin with. His place lies over there." Mayne pointed through an opening in the trees to the wooded heights. "It's called Abbotside, you know; the house was an abbey in old times, and can boast of a ghost or two. It's always crammed with people as soon as the town season is over; Lady Rexbury is fond of society, and mothers with marriageable daughters are all struggling for Lord Wyburn."

"How vulgar of them to struggle," said Nelly, with a very good imitation of Lady Florence's manner. "And are any of these desperate strugglers successful!"

"Oh, Lord Wyburn won't marry yet," replied Mayne, laughing. "He'll put off the evil day as long as he can. He manages to amuse himself pretty well."

"I have heard of him," Nelly said, after a pause. "Very fast, isn't he?"

"Rather beyond the average, I believe," Mayne admitted. "He will have something to look at next Sunday. His mother and her guests will stare at you, my dear; and it will rejoice their hearts to hear that you belong to me."

"I don't want to belong to any one else," said Nelly, nestling close to her lover.

"Darling," he answered, "we shall spend a life-time together."

"Only a life-time; it's such a little while!" the girl murmured. "I wish we could live always."

At that moment, when the sun shone on them through the boughs, and his cheek was pressed to hers, Mayne could readily have prayed for an earthly immortality. When men and women are young and beautiful and happy in a first love, it is hard to believe that the soul can ever long to escape from the tenement that seems so fair. The bird sings; the lips we love give us kiss for kiss; surely it is a sweet thing to live "while the evil days come not, nor the years draw nigh, when thou shalt say, I have no pleasure in them."

For a little while they were silent. Mayne knew that his people disapproved of his choice, and Nelly suspected that she was not welcome at the manor, but both had forgotten it in that blissful hush. A bird rustled in the leaves overhead; the girl released herself, and then sighed.

They went slowly back to the house to dress for dinner, and Nelly ran up at once to her own room. Looking far away, across the hills and woods, she caught sight of a church spire rising above the trees. Farther off still there was a glimpse of grey towers against a golden sky.

"That is Abbeyside," she thought. "I wonder if Lady Rexbury will ask us to dine? No, I suppose not; I don't think Susie and Phyllis would interest the 'smart people' very much," she added, curving her rich red lips in a scornful little smile. "They haven't a word to say for themselves, and they are not pretty enough to sit silent and be looked at."

And Nelly sighed again, but this was a different kind of sigh.

They could find no fault with her when she came down to dinner. Her dress was not too fine for her position; she wore no jewels; a bunch of her favourite scarlet flowers was her sole adornment. And yet they were all saying in their inmost hearts that this strange girl was too beautiful, too fashionable, and far too self-possessed to be a poor governess.

CHAPTER VII.

TALKING IT OVER.

"The wild and wizard beauty of her race."

LONGFELLOW

THE ladies of the manor were old-fashioned in their ways and went early to rest. The father and son had repaired to the library to smoke a pipe together; and Mrs. Comberford, instead of going straight to her own apartment, had paused in Susie's room to talk over the events of the day with her daughters.

The walls of the old house were thick; Nelly

was sleeping on the other side of the gallery, and yet they instinctively lowered their voices.

Susie was at the looking-glass, brushing her hair, and half enveloped in its silky fairness. She had a noble face, not beautiful, but trustworthy; and there was a look of steadfast truth in her deep-set blue eyes. On the side of the bed sat Phyllis, two years younger, long-limbed and slender; her features not so boldly chiselled as her sister's, her face paler in its heavy folds of fair hair. Leaning against the foot of the bedstead she looked up at her mother with an anxious gaze.

" But are you *quite* sure that Nelly is a gipsy?" she asked.

Susie paused, brush in hand, to speak a word of caution.

" Hush, Phyllis, not so loud. Of course mother can't be quite sure; so little is really known."

" Not a syllable must be said before Madge and

Rosa," Mrs. Comberford answered warningly.
"Don't mention the word gipsy in their presence.
It's a dreadful word," she added, with a slight
shiver.

"But gipsies are to be found everywhere in
society, according to Mr. Leland," said Susie.
"They are to be met with in palaces as well
as in tents. Go where you will, though you
may not know it, you encounter them in one
form or the other at every step. If we had
not been told the story of Nelly's babyhood
we should not have suspected her origin."

"I think I should have suspected it," Mrs.
Comberford replied. "There is a curious witchery about her; a peculiar grace and suppleness
which mark her descent. She looks picturesque
in anything that she puts on."

"She isn't so very dark, you know;—quite
a light shade of brunette," said Phyllis consolingly.

"Oh, I don't care about her complexion,"
sighed the poor mother. "It is the indescrib-

able charm about her which tells what she is;
—a wicked charm I call it. I am sure she
has bewitched my poor boy!"

Susie coiled up her fair hair with firm white
fingers, and the candle-light revealed a shadow
of trouble on her face.

"Dear mother," she said, "every young man
is bewitched—to a certain extent—when he is in
love."

"No, Susie, not when he falls in love in a
natural, wholesome way. I was a nice-looking
girl when your father courted me, and he was
very fond of me; but he wasn't bewitched."

Susie mentally acknowledged that there was
common-sense in this reply. She was young
and had not seen much of the world; but being
a thoughtful girl she had studied those small
portions of it that came within her ken.
Observation and reflection had taught her that
there are two kinds of love,—the love that
supports, and the love that enslaves. Her father

had wooed a woman who was lady-love and help-meet in one. But would Nelly—dazzling, charming Nelly—ever help a man to tread those rugged places which must come in the course of every life-journey? She was the kind of girl whose youth is a triumphal march;—a girl for whom many a lance would have been broken in the old tournament times, and many a bumper drained when toasting beauties was the order of the day. But it required an effort of the imagination to picture her as the wife of a man with a limited income, busy with the old prosaic struggle to make two ends meet.

"Father's love was the right love," she said, after a moment's pause. And then she went over to her mother and gave her a kiss.

"Yes, it was the right love, my dear," Mrs. Comberford answered tenderly. "He said yesterday—'I hope my son will be as happy in his choice as I have been in mine'."

"John Bunyan was a gipsy; father says so,"

remarked Phyllis in a meditative tone. "They are not fools, are they? I daresay there's much to be said in their favour, but I don't fancy them, myself. And I wish poor dear Angela had never been at school with Nelly;—it was Angela who began it all."

"Wishing won't alter the matter," Susie replied. "We must make the best of it. And, after all, we are not *quite* sure that Nelly has any gipsy blood in her. Let us get all the comfort out of the doubt that we can."

Mrs. Comberford sighed heavily.

"And even if it's as bad as our fears," said Phyllis, "we can't be expected to know all our connections by marriage. How funny to have a sister-in-law related to the old fortune-teller who stole those spoons last year! And the man in the fur cap who made so free with our hens!"

"Be quiet, Phyllis," whispered Susie.

"Nelly's relations may be almost as troublesome as Undine's," the girl went on. "Do you remember the terrible uncle Kühleborn?"

Mrs. Comberford rose wearily to go to her own room. She kissed her daughters, and went away, shutting the door softly behind her.

"Phyllis," said Susie gravely, "you must not joke about Nelly's origin. Don't you see that the mother is deeply distressed? She has taken this matter to heart."

"Well, I'm sorry that Mayne is engaged. We were much happier when he wasn't," Phyllis answered. "But nothing will ever make him give her up. She is so wonderfully pretty, you know."

"We used to laugh when poor Angela went into raptures over her friend," Susie said sadly. "Who could foresee that we should all be dazzled and bewildered by that very girl? I want to love her for Mayne's sake, and yet I can't help sympathizing with mother. She has family pride; and father too——"

"Oh, father isn't well pleased, although he doesn't say much," exclaimed Phyllis. "But, after all, why do we make such a fuss? They can't marry for years, and there's many a slip between the cup and the lip."

"I don't like that saying; it's horrid, Phyllis. I'd rather think that we shall all learn to love Nelly, and overcome our prejudice. She cannot help her birth, poor girl; and it was very right of her to tell all that she knew of herself so frankly. I mean to make her love me, if I can; but I'm afraid I was stiff to-day. She was such a surprise."

"Well, good night." Phyllis spoke in a softer tone, as she rose from her seat on the bed. "I'm quite willing to love her, Susie; only it's so disquieting to see mother fretting."

She passed through the door which led from her sister's room into her own. This door was never closed; it stood open all night. The Comberford girls had always been united; and since Angela's death Susie and Phyllis seemed to have but one heart between them.

Left to herself, Susie sat down in a chair by the toilet-table and opened a little red-edged book of devotions. But she had not read more than one sentence when Phyllis the irrepressible put her head in at the door again.

"Oh Susie, how shall we parry all Christina Payton's questions? She will call to-morrow,—see if she doesn't?—and she will ask who Nelly's father is, and if she is like her mother, and if one of her brothers isn't in the 190th foot? Christina always introduces that regiment into her conversation; she has a cousin in it, you know, and he is the sole link that connects her with military life. It's astonishing how great a strain one tiny link will bear! It will be splendid fun to hear Nelly's answers, and to see Christina's little narrow eyes twinkling with curiosity and rage. Yes, rage. Don't stop me, Susie; you know quite well that Christina would be willing to marry Mayne on sixpence a week. And I'd rather have a sister-in-law straight·from a gipsy's tent than Christina Payton."

"Do go to bed, Phyllis," said Susie, with tired patience in her voice. "Christina has done nothing to make you dislike her so much. It's very wrong of you to say such unkind things of her. She has always been kind to us all, and mother has a regard for her, I know. Now *do* go to bed."

CHAPTER VIII.

A LOVE GIFT.

"A thing stuck on with oaths upon your finger,
And riveted so with faith unto your flesh.
THE MERCHANT OF VENICE.

IN the library the talk between Mayne and his father had been pleasant enough. Mr. Comberford had praised Nelly's beauty and grace, and had carefully refrained from uttering a word which might wound the feelings of his son.

The boy had been a good boy, he said to himself; and it often goes ill with a young man when his heart's first love is denied to him. It is true that he, too, had a share of that old-fashioned family pride which flourishes in country solitudes, and decays in the atmosphere of cities; but he had done his best to smooth away his wife's irritation. "It is always the mother who is hardest to please," he had said smilingly to Mayne. "And if you had brought us a princess your mother would scarcely have thought her good enough for her lad."

Mayne had laughed pleasantly, and had avowed a decided disinclination for an august alliance.

"I'd rather my wife should look up to me than down on me," he said. "Now that we have touched on this subject, father, I want to say that Nelly and I are quite prepared to wait. She isn't at all anxious to marry on youth and good looks and vague expectations. Moreover, the Camdens can't spare her yet. She has a good home with them, you see; and she can stay there in comfort till she comes to me."

"I'm glad you are both so sensible." Mr. Comberford spoke in a tone of relief. "Not that I wish you to wait too long; and if it were in my power to shorten the waiting-time I would gladly do it. But I have a good deal of faith in old Cottrell, Mayne, in spite of all the nonsense he writes about magic and moonshine. And I think he'll clear the way for you."

"Magic and moonshine," Mayne repeated, laughing. "Do you know that wouldn't be a bad title for a book?"

"Then write the book, by all means," said his father.

"That's more easily said than done, sir, isn't it?"

"I don't know. I have sometimes had a vague notion that you could write a book if you tried. You have plenty of imagination, Mayne, and you're always reading. Wasn't it Sir Walter Scott who said he was a greedy reader? I've seen you, when you were a very small kid, devouring books that were never intended for kids at all."

"Oh, I've had my dreams of authorship," Mayne confessed gaily. "But they are over now. When a man means to get married and settled, and become a respectable member of society, he must put away dreams. By the way, I wish I knew exactly what I was going to do when old Cottrell has done with me."

"So do I, my boy," said Mr. Comberford, with a sigh. "But I can only repeat that I've faith in Cottrell. He knows scores of influential people, and he'll get a berth for you one of these days."

"And for the present I'm provided for. Well, sir, we won't look at the gloomy side of life to-night."

Mayne went up to his room—the room which he had always occupied when a boy,—and thought over the day from beginning to end. He was a little angry with his mother and the girls; were they going to spoil Nelly's visit with their stiff ways?

But when he sought his pillow his anger died away in a confusion of sweet images. He loved, and she loved him, and their future life was bathed in glorious light. Such a love as his was immortal; he had no fear of disenchantment, no dread of satiety.

The short August night wore away. Then there was the cool stir of the morning wind in the tree-tops, and the early sunbeams crept in through Nelly's window. She woke quietly, and lay still in a dreamy mood, drinking in the sweetness of the jessamine scent that filled the room. The lattice had been left unfastened all night long, and the dewy perfumes of the dawn came in with the first light.

She was very happy, but—— Why is there always a "but" when we think about our happiness? Of course Mrs. Comberford would always detest her, Nelly thought. The girls might be won over to her side; the mother never. Nelly believed that she could read the signs of unconquerable aversion in the matron's deep-blue eyes, which scanned her with such a cold, steady gaze.

If she had made up some pretty little fiction about her babyhood, and had left out the gipsies altogether, she might have had a more cordial reception. Nelly began to think that it was a mistake to tell the unvarnished truth. The truth, what was it? Something that was only spoken by fools and children.

It must be early; breakfast-time was still far distant, she supposed; but oh, how hungry she was! This fresh morning air was a strong tonic indeed. Just then, there was a knock; the door opened gently, and Susie appeared, carrying a small tray. Nelly's eyes were gladdened by the sight of a quaint little china tea-pot, a cream-jug, and some slices of brown bread-and-butter.

"How kind you are!" she said, rewarding Mayne's sister with a bright smile. "But why do you wait upon me?"

Susie smiled too, but her face clouded for a moment. "We have had losses," she answered, "so Phyllis and I do all that we can in the house. We always rise early; and I have taken mother's tea into her room. Did you sleep well?"

"Very well," said Nelly gratefully.

Susie looked admiringly at the richly-tinted face, set in a crumpled mass of dark-brown hair, and wondered at its flowery freshness. Nelly did not look in the least like a jaded Londoner. After all, it was easy to love any one so beautiful and gracious as this poor stranger was; and Susie felt that her own prejudice was melting like snow before the sun.

"Don't get up until you feel inclined to move," she said. "I'm glad you have had a good night, and I hope you will have a happy day."

Something simple and sweet seemed to flow into Nelly's heart and fill it to the brim that morning. She felt, as she rose and dressed, that she had come here to claim a half-forgotten kinship with the flowers and the birds. Life was full of blossom and song; in this country paradise there were no discordant notes; every hour was filled with perfect melody; every gap was overgrown with green.

All the doors of the old house were set wide open to let the balmy air wander in. There was the scent of the woods and pastures everywhere, and sometimes a strong breath of pine fragrance would come from a neighbouring plantation. Mayne was standing at the foot of the stairs, waiting for Nelly.

His handsome face had a summer glow upon

it, and his fair hair, close cropped, caught the light on its crisp waves. He had been out early into the fields, and had brought in a bunch of splendid scarlet poppies.

"See what I have got for you!" he said, as she ran lightly down to him. "You are never contented without a bit of red, you know."

She separated two or three flowers from the bunch, and, stepping up to the glass above the hat-stand, proceeded to arrange them in her dress. It was a simple gown enough, made of brown holland, and trimmed with lace of the same hue; but the poppies gave it a touch of sumptuous colour. Just for a moment she stood and surveyed herself with the satisfied air which comes naturally to a pretty girl in front of a mirror. Mayne stood behind her, looking over her shoulder.

At that instant Mrs. Comberford came out of the dining-room, and looked sharply at the charming figure before the glass. Mayne saw the look, and resented it as any lover would have done. There was a cold, keen dislike in his mother's blue eyes, an expression new and strange, which seemed, somehow, to put a sense of distance between her and himself. He hoped that Nelly had not seen it.

But she had; Nelly was a girl who saw everything.

She 'moved away from the glass, quickly, yet gracefully, and turned to her hostess with a sunny smile. Until then, Nelly had never known what a difficult process smiling is under certain circumstances. Nevertheless she accomplished her smile creditably.

"I never saw such lovely poppies anywhere else," she said. "One might fancy that they grew in fairy-land."

Mrs. Comberford was not a good actress. In all her simple matronly life there had been little need of feigning anything. There was a croak in her voice when she answered Nelly, and it sounded harsh even in her own ears.

"We have beautiful wild flowers here," she forced herself to say.

"Come to breakfast," said Mayne, putting his arm round Nelly's waist, and leading her into the room. He avoided his mother's eyes; and she knew that she had offended him. Instead of taking any blame to herself she only thought bitterly "that it was all that girl's fault. She had come into the family to make mischief."

But Mayne and Nelly had almost forgotten that unkindly glance when they rambled out into the garden after breakfast. It was a very old-fashioned garden with lily walks and hedges of clipped yews; and a man who did his courting there ought to have worn a prune-coloured coat, knee-breeches, and a lace cravat. But Mayne played his part well enough in a prosaic suit of light tweed and a straw hat.

"Oh, Mayne, I have never had a ring before!" she said in a tone of delight. "And this is splendid,

—such a rich, deep red,—a ruby, isn't it?"

"Yes, a ruby,—'a drop of my heart's blood', you know. You are such a superstitious little darling that I daresay you believe it will bring you good fortune."

"Of course I believe that," Nelly answered. "It will keep away ill dreams, and it's a charm against the evil eye."

"You silliest of pets; no one here has such a thing as an evil eye."

"So much the better," she said, suddenly recalling his mother's glance. "Nevertheless, I'm glad I have a safeguard. Only, dear Mayne, I think this ring is far too costly for a poor little governess."

"Nothing is too costly for you, my darling," he answered fervently.

"Nothing, Mayne? Not even 'a drop of your heart's blood'?"

"Not even every drop of blood in my body, Nelly."

With the August sun shining over that old garden, the warm air full of rich odours and bird-voices, it was the very paradise for a pair of ardent lovers. The man and the girl, standing together under the shade of an ancient pear-tree, were looking their handsomest at this moment; the light flickered down on Nelly's pretty dress and mellow cheek as she lifted her dark eyes to his with the perfect assurance of open and requited love.

"What a sanguinary declaration," she said, suddenly breaking into a musical little laugh. "But I hope I shall never cost you anything more, dear Mayne. No more presents, remember! We are a needy young couple, you know; and one splendid gift is enough for a life-time."

The words came back to him afterwards with a meaning which she had not given them. She did not realize how high a price he had really paid for her ring, nor suspect the sacrifice that he had made to obtain it. He had parted with several cherished possessions to buy the ruby which seemed the most fitting gift for the girl he loved. And it was only a type of that other gift—"the one splendid gift" which is indeed enough for a life-time,—the first great love of a man's heart.

They went off together into the cornfields, and trod the narrow paths running through the russet gold. And so the bright morning glided away.

CHAPTER IX.

THE GREEN-EYED MONSTER.

Shall some one deck thee over and down,
Up and about with blossoms and leaves?
Fix his heart's fruit for thy garland crown,
Cling with his soul as the gourd-vine cleaves?
                                        ROBERT BROWNING.

SUNDAY came; and Nelly, as she prepared for church, was not unmindful of all those "smart people" who were expected to be there.

Mayne, when he looked at her, thought tenderly of the bright Sunday morning when he had seen her first in Lincoln's Inn. The old chapel, away in London, was hallowed by that first vision of his love; and now that she was his own, openly acknowledged as belonging to him, he found a curious pleasure in recalling the day when she had seemed more like a glorious dream than a reality. Meanwhile Nelly, as she walked by his side, was wondering whether any one would find out that her soft grey gown was a little faded here and there? Her gloves were quite perfect, she said to herself; and nobody would peep between the folds of her dress. Her bonnet, too, was irreproachable.

The church was small and dim; but there was no lack of light in the chancel, where the seats were appropriated by the leading members of the congregation. The manor pew was exactly opposite to that which was occupied by Lord Rexbury and his family. The earl's pew

was long,—very long—and filled with ladies,
who stared with languid curiosity at Nelly and
the Comberford girls. There were two vacant
places left at one end, and these were not taken
till the service had just begun. Then Lord
Rexbury and his son came in together.

The earl was a tall, lean man, with round
shoulders, and a worried, fretful look on his
face. Lord Wyburn, much shorter than his
father, had a sallow-fair complexion, and a
whitey-brown moustache. His eyes, small and
restless, were light grey; his nose was small,
too; but the lips, half hidden under the moustache, were full, and the jaw was heavy. He
was not a pleasant-looking young man; he had
none of that knightliness which romantic people
associate with an ancient name. He did not
possess the kind of face that would have looked
well under a casque and nodding plume, nor
could you have imagined him in the long locks
and feathered hat of a cavalier. And yet, unat-

tractive as he was, Nelly's beautiful eyes regarded him with a deeper interest than she chose to show.

He was Lord Wyburn. For two seasons he had been courted and flattered and run after in vain. Lady Florence had laughed good-humouredly at the ineffectual attempts to captivate him which many of her young friends had made. Nelly had read his name repeatedly in the society journals which were scattered about in the Camdens' house, and she was fully aware of his importance in the fashionable world. And so, although handsome Mayne, her plighted lover, was standing by her side, she felt a thrill of satisfaction when Lord Wyburn's glance rested on her face.

If a man looked at Nelly once, he was sure to look again. That exquisite face, with its soft, mellow tints, could not fail to attract him as ripe fruit attracts a child.

Lord Wyburn *did* look again, not once,

but many times. So often did he look, in fact, that Mayne began to grow hot and restless; and even Mr. Comberford glanced uneasily at his future daughter-in-law. But Nelly seemed perfectly unconscious that she was attracting any notice at all.

There she stood, the picture of innocent loveliness, holding her prayer-book quietly in her delicately-gloved hands; there were no ungraceful starts and fidgets, no signs of self-consciousness. And yet there was not a single member of the Comberford family who did not observe Lord Wyburn's admiration, which, without being offensively displayed, was quite evident. Mrs. Comberford resented it keenly.

"It must be *her* fault," she thought. "He guesses that she likes to be admired."

But even her prejudiced eyes could detect no flaw in the smooth perfection of Nelly's demeanour.

Mayne, chafing and fuming in secret, was

longing for the service to come to an end.
He had not brought Nelly here that Lord
Wyburn might feast his ugly eyes upon her.
Old Payton was preaching one of his longest
sermons, too; and preaching it in the droning
self-satisfied voice which was sure to rouse the
ire of an irritable hearer. Christina Payton was
staring, first at Lord Wyburn and then at
Nelly;—why was everybody behaving in this
maddening way?

Aiming an irrepressible kick at the hassock,
Mayne's foot came with a bang against the
panel of the pew. All the Comberfords started
visibly; and Phyllis, betraying an inclination to
giggle, received a smart tap of admonition
from her mother. The tap made matters worse,
and the giggle very nearly ended in an explosion
of laughter through the nose. Poor Susie,
growing crimson, gave her sister's gown a pull,
hardly knowing what the effect of this mute
remonstrance would be. And Nelly, her calm

still unruffled, sat peacefully, through all the turmoil.

"And now," said Mr. Payton coming to the end of his last page. They all rose with alacrity, Mayne registering a mental vow that he would never bring Nelly here again while that beast was at Abbeyside. Meanwhile the beast ma-nœuvred, not unskilfully, to get close to the new beauty as she came out of the pew.

He was successful; in spite of all Mayne's vigilance he was successful; but it could not be supposed for a moment that he was helped in the slightest degree by Nelly herself. When they reached the church door a slight shower was falling, and it is true that the dear girl turned artlessly round to look for Mayne, who chanced to be on the other side. This swift movement brought her face to face with Lord Wyburn, and very nearly precipitated her into his arms.

Nobody could blame her of course. Mrs.

Comberford, who had been fortunately seized upon by a neighbour, did not witness this trifling incident; but Susie and Phyllis did.

"Come, Nelly, here's an umbrella," said Mayne, taking possession of his betrothed with great promptness. "The rain is nothing at all; it will be over in another minute."

He held the umbrella over her in a fashion which completely shielded her from further observation. Her hand was on his arm, and she found herself half led, half carried along a narrow gravelled path with green mounds on the right and left. Almost breathless, she was borne out of the churchyard into a shady lane, and saw that most of the congregation were left behind.

"Oh Mayne," she panted, "how you have hurried me! We might have waited for the others."

"No," he said sternly. "I wouldn't leave you near that hideous little brute a second longer."

She looked up at him with a swift, bright look, meeting his gaze frankly enough.

"Where was the hideous little brute?" she asked in her innocent voice.

"Where?" His face was still hot with temper. "Facing you all through the service, and staring in a way that made me long to kick him."

"I think you must have kicked him in imagination," she remarked quietly. "Did you hear the noise you made in church? Robby behaves better than you do."

He looked subdued.

"I lost patience," he confessed after a pause. "And old Payton was no end of a bore. But that fellow Wyburn, Nelly,—did you see how he followed you?"

"You have got him on the brain," she answered in a pitying tone. "My dear Mayne, he will forget my existence before he has had his lunch. Why do you worry yourself about trifles?"

"Was it a trifle?" he asked.

She felt rather than saw the deep-blue eyes and mobile lips set in an expression of sternness. And then he added in a softer tone,

"I don't think, dear, there are any trifles in love."

"Oh yes, there are," replied the girl brightly.

> "'Trifles, light as air,
> Are to the jealous confirmations strong
> As proofs of holy writ.'

"Come, Mayne, let us join the others. What will your mother think of us when she finds we have vanished? This is a sort of by-path leading to nowhere, isn't it?"

"We must climb this stile, and take a short cut across the downs," he answered. "We shall get home as soon as they do. Nelly, I was right in what I said just now. Love carries a magnifying glass, so that there are no trifles to him."

"Dear me, I didn't know he carried a magnifying glass," said Nelly gaily. "He would be much prettier without it. I've only seen him with his bow and arrows."

She climbed the stile lightly as she spoke; but he had vaulted over it first, and took her into his arms.

"Now," he said, holding her fast as she stood on the step above him. "Now you shall quiet all my doubts and fears with a kiss."

"That would be encouraging you to doubt again. You will always be doubting and getting quieted," she answered, bringing her radiant face just a little nearer to his.

The light rain had left a few diamonds hanging on the dwarf bushes; a sweet coolness sighed through the sultry noontide, and soft cloud shadows flitted over the sunny downs. The young pair climbed the slopes with nimble feet, laughing when the sheep sped away at their approach, and hurried over the short grass with

tiny tinklings of little bells. Mayne had quite
got over his annoyance when they reached
the manor; but his face clouded again at the
sight of an unexpected guest.

"Christina joined us after service, and mother
asked her to lunch," said Susie, meeting the
lovers at the gate.

"Why was she asked to lunch?" Mayne
demanded irritably.

"Hush, she may hear you. She has a plan
for a picnic, and she wants to discuss it with
us."

Miss Payton was a tall woman, taller even
than the Comberford girls, and decidedly thin.
There was some reason to find fault with her
eyes, which were, as Phyllis had said, small
and narrow, and had something furtive in their
glances. But, without being pretty, Christina
was rather nice-looking. She had contrived to
gain a certain amount of popularity among the
county people; and had a little money, a hundred

a year or more;—— and if Mayne had happened to think of her, Mrs. Comberford would
not have quarrelled with his choice.

Mayne had neither liked nor disliked her;
he had simply accepted her as a part of his life
at Hartside. He had played with her when
he was a boy in knickerbockers and she a
girl in a long pinafore, one year older than
himself. But, after his engagement with Nelly
was announced at home, there was a change
in his feeling to Christina Payton.

Mrs. Comberford, exasperated by the idea of
having Nelly for a daughter-in-law, had let slip
some foolish words which could not be recalled.
She had said with a burst of tears,

"I wish, with all my heart, that you had
chosen Christina. I should have known then
that you would have a wife who could be depended
upon. At any rate Christina is a lady, and she
was born in a decent house, and not under a
hedge."

A most unwise speech was this; Mrs. Comberford was heartily sorry that she had uttered it, and had tried to atone for it with a motherly kiss. But Mayne, although he had almost forgiven his mother for that unlucky outburst, was unjust enough to lay the blame of it on the shoulders of his old play-mate.

Christina, he said to himself, was a girl who had nasty sly ways, and she had crept into his mother's favour in a designing fashion. He did not disclose these thoughts to his sisters; but the Comberfords seemed to understand each other without words. And Susie, when she went to meet the young couple at the gate, was quite sure that Mayne would resent Christina's presence at lunch.

"Oh, we don't want a picnic," he muttered with a frown. But Nelly looked up with sunny eyes, and asked if it would not be very nice?

"I haven't been to a picnic since I was a girl at school;" she remarked.

"That's a very long time ago,—twenty years at least," said Mayne, won back to good humour. "I think we must go, if only to remind you of your vanished youth."

After having seen the meeting at the railway station Christina had divined the truth. Mayne was engaged; even the vicar, who was not by any means a man of quick perceptions, had come to that conclusion.

On the Saturday following Nelly's arrival Miss Payton had shut herself up with a headache. It was a headache that made her eyes red and her cheeks pale; and her father and mother had tact enough to take very little notice of her indisposition. When Sunday came she was well again, active and alert; and had attached herself to Mrs. Comberford as they came out of church.

"I know what has happened," she said cheerfully to her old friend. "Mayne has got engaged to some one he has met in London. Dear Mrs. Comberford, how lovely she is! Are you very much delighted? Do tell me all about her."

If Mayne's mother had taken lessons of my Lady Feigning, it would have been better for her at this trying moment. But to dissemble was, as we know, beyond her skill.

"There is little to tell," she answered in a constrained voice. "She is a Miss Stanley, our dear Angela's school-friend."

"What, the Nelly Stanley who was such a paragon?" cried Christina, with animation. "How very interesting! He has not known her long, I suppose?"

"Not long," Mrs. Comberford replied. "The affair took us all by surprise. He is very happy, and very much in love; and he has brought her here to spend her holidays."

"Her holidays? Then she is a teacher at Angela's old college?"

"No," Mrs. Comberford strove to hide her mortification. "She is a governess in a family in Russell Square."

"Oh," said Christina, in a gentle tone. She put no more questions, but began to speak about the picnic. And Mrs. Comberford asked her to lunch.

In spite of Mayne's ill-will towards the vicar's daughter, he could find no fault with her manner that day. She met Nelly with frank kindness, and spoke with feeling about Angela, and the school friendship. All was going smoothly; there were no impertinent inquiries; no sarcastic remarks; and the afternoon had nearly glided away when Miss Payton ruffled somebody's plumes at last.

"What did you think of Lord Wyburn, Miss Stanley?" she suddenly asked.

Nelly could feel that Mayne started.

"He did not interest me in the least," she answered.

"Didn't he? I thought perhaps you had met him somewhere. He was looking at you all through the service."

"Was he? I suppose I am like some one he knows;" said Nelly, with perfect composure.

CHAPTER X.

A TIFF.

So true a fool is love, that in your will
(Though you do anything) he thinks no ill.
SHAKSPEARE.

"I WONDER if Christina really wanted to annoy Mayne?" said Phyllis to her sister that night.

As usual, the two girls were talking confidentially before they went to rest. Until Nelly came they had had nothing to talk about beyond the ordinary routine of their duties, and the new books which they were reading. But Nelly had flashed into this sober household like some bright visitant from another sphere; and the quiet inmates of the manor were living in a state of excitement.

"I hope not," Susie answered. "It was

inconsiderate of her to say anything about Lord Wyburn's glances. But perhaps she doesn't realize that Mayne is very easily upset just now."

They were both silent for a moment. Then Phyllis shook back her long hair with an impatient gesture and spoke almost pettishly.

"It seems to me that his love-affair does him more harm than good. He gets only a fitful kind of happiness out of it," she said. "He used to be the best-tempered fellow in the world, but to-day he looked quite savage. Will it always be like this?"

"Oh no; it won't always be like this. Such a state of mind cannot last," Susie replied.

"But it will do a great deal of mischief while it does last," Phyllis said. "I'm afraid that his is not the right kind of love, or that Nelly isn't the right kind of girl to be loved. It must be very uncomfortable to be in love with a girl who attracts so much attention."

"It's a pity that he is so over-sensitive about

her," Susie admitted sadly. "But I think the over-sensitiveness will wear off. This is the first love-affair in our family, you know; and it disturbs our peace."

"I hope I shan't be a nuisance when my turn comes. However, nobody will ever be as distracted about me as Mayne is about Nelly," remarked Phyllis in a tone of conviction. "Did you notice the splendid ruby ring that she is wearing? He must have spent all that he had upon it."

"I wish he had given her something less costly," said Susie, with a sigh. "There is an extravagance about this love of his. Poor dear boy, he reminds me of Romeo.

"'These violent delights have violent ends,
    And in their triumph die.'"

"But there was no Rosaline before he wooed this Juliet," cried Phyllis. "Nelly is his first love; he never cared a sou for any other girl,

and so he pours out all the accumulated devotion of his youth at her feet. How admirably
I express myself, Susie! It's too bad that such
eloquence should be wasted on the desert air
of this bed-room. Good night."

And with a dramatic wave of the hand, Phyllis went off into her own apartment, leaving her
sister still sitting thoughtfully at the toilet-table.

On Monday morning the girls decided that it
was time to gather the plums,—those large golden
plums for which the manor orchard was famed.
Nelly, who was in high spirits, begged for a
basket that she might help in picking up the fruit
that fell. And Mayne volunteered to climb the
trees.

Nelly's gaiety was infectious. Susie, who had
come down to breakfast in a sober mood, was
beguiled into mirth; and Phyllis, who loved fun,
chattered and laughed as if her home life had
never known a cloud.

The orchard was only divided from the road

by a low hedge; and a horseman, riding along at a leisurely pace, could get a distinct view of the three girlish figures under the trees. As the sound of hoofs drew nearer, Nelly sprang laughingly away from her companions to pursue a black kitten which bounded off in the direction of the hedge. Lord Wyburn, mounted on his favourite chestnut, saw the very face which had haunted his dreams confronting him in the sunny morning light. Her brown eyes shone upon him for a moment; he caught a glimpse of richly-glowing cheeks, and crimson lips parted in a smile; and then she turned and went springing back to the others.

They received her in silence. From the tree in which Mayne was standing, embowered in leaves, they had heard a muttered curse; and their spirits sank within them.

A shadow seemed to have fallen over the brightness of the morning. The sisters tried to laugh at Nelly's gay speeches; but all the merriment had died out of their hearts. They piled up plums in the baskets with listless hands, and presently Susie carried her basketful into the house. Phyllis followed ; and Mayne swung himself down from the tree.

"Upon my word, Nelly," he began, "this is a great deal too bad! I make every allowance for a man who has got into the habit of running after pretty faces, but when all is said and done, one does expect decent behaviour from a gentleman."

"Oh, you are beginning about Lord Wyburn again." She was far too wise to pretend that she did not understand him. "Hasn't he a right to ride on the queen's highway ?"

There was something mutinous in her soft voice, and her rich bloom had deepened.

"But he has no right to stare into another man's orchard," cried Mayne. "He rode here to get another glimpse of you, and you must needs reward him for his pains!"

He thrust his hands into his pockets, and took short marches under the plum-tree. His handsome face was darkened with anger and distress, —very real anger and distress as Nelly could see at a glance.

His hat had fallen off, and was lying on the grass at her feet. She picked it up and went quietly to his side.

"Don't rampage, Mayne;" she said, laying her hand gently on his arm. "I think I ought to be angry with you, but I'm not;—not very. I won't believe that you really accuse me of running to the hedge to let Lord Wyburn look at me. If you did——"

She paused suddenly. Her lips were compressed, and she seemed to be struggling with some strong feeling not easy to overcome. He looked at her and found himself subdued.

"What a brute I am," he burst out. "How absurd all this is! There I was, cursing up in the tree, and spoiling the pleasure of those two poor girls, all because that ugly little satyr came prowling near our grounds."

"Exactly," assented Nelly promptly. "You can't prevent his prowling, you see. It's a way that satyrs have, I suppose. Nobody wants to see them; they're not pretty to look at, but somehow they intrude themselves upon you at every turn. For my own part, I wish the race was extinct; but what can one do?"

And thus the little scene ended. The pair returned to the house with cloudless faces, and Nelly gaily claimed her share of the plums. But she could not quite succeed in winning Susie back to her side that day.

Susie Comberford was a girl who had strange premonitions; flashes of insight; swift revelations of other people's inmost selves; and so it came to pass that she saw more than she wanted to see. She liked Nelly already, and was beginning to feel that she should learn, in time, to love her. And yet she did not quite believe in her.

The artlessness and utter indifference to admiration were unreal; the affection for Mayne,
although real, was not an adequate return for
the devotion which, as Phyllis had lackadaisically
said, he poured at her feet.

Susie understood her brother, and knew that
there were depths in his nature which he had
never sounded yet.   She was a young girl; but
she had read and thought more deeply than
girls generally do.   She took life seriously—too
seriously, some said; and there was always about
her something of the

> ———"pensive nun, devout and pure,
> Sober, steadfast, and demure."

Without being steeped in self-consciousness,
and given up to self-analysis like poor Marie
Bashkirtseff, Susie studied her inner life, and
often judged herself as an accusing angel might
have done.   For other people, however, she
was always ready to find excuses; and if no

excuse could possibly be found, she covered their sins with silence.

She did not want to judge Nelly. But she knew the sudden pursuit of the black kitten had been cleverly timed. Nelly's bright eyes had caught a glimpse of the approaching rider, and she had yielded at once to the impulse to see and be seen. If Lord Wyburn had admired her in the dim church, he should know that her beauty could stand the test of blazing sunshine. It was a natural impulse, perhaps, and not altogether blameworthy; but a true love would have conquered it, just for true love's sake.

"The picnic is to come off on Friday," said Mrs. Comberford as they sat at luncheon. "Christina's invitations have all been accepted. I am not going; you young people can be trusted to take care of yourselves, and there is Mrs. Payton to look after you."

"Are we to go?" asked little Madge eagerly.

"No, dear; the grown-up people won't want

you," the mother answered. "But you shall have a picnic made up of little ones before Nelly leaves us. We will have a grand feast in the pine wood, and plenty of fun."

"And hear fairy stories afterwards," cried Madge in delight. "Do you know any good fairy stories, Nelly? Mayne's tales are lovely, but he isn't always in the mood to tell them."

"They don't come to me unless I am in the mood," Mayne said, laughing.

"I hope the mood will come while I'm here," remarked Nelly. "Robby makes great demands upon my imagination. I should like to store up some of your stories for his benefit."

"Tell us more about Louie and Robby," pleaded little Rose, when they were leaving the table. And Nelly went out with the children willingly enough, and sat under the shade of the great cedar to amuse them for half an hour.

"What a good-natured girl she is," said

Mr. Comberford to his wife. "It's a good sign when children take kindly to a woman. How the little ones used to flock round you, Kate, in the old days!"

"I never had Nelly's witchery," Mrs. Comberford replied, half sadly. "Mine were simple, motherly ways which came to me by nature. Our children look upon Nelly as some one out of the fairy tales they are so fond of. She is like an enchantress."

"She's a sweet creature," said Mr. Comberford, watching the pretty group under the cedar. "Our Mayne might have made a worse choice."

"Sometimes, Henry, I am sorry that he didn't choose poor Christina," said the wife with a swift glance at her husband's face. "She has always been a favourite of mine; and we know her so well, you see, that Mayne's engagement with her would have seemed the most natural thing in the world."

"There has never been the least chance

of such a thing, Kate. Mayne is a romantic fellow;—just the kind of fellow to roam far afield in search of a rare flower. And he has found it."

"Yes, he has found it. But rare flowers don't always thrive when they are planted in home gardens. It is best to choose a plant that will take naturally to the soil in which it has to grow."

Mr. Comberford did not care to pursue the subject. His face wore a look which his wife understood well enough. It was a look that expressed his dislike to hear disparaging remarks about Nelly.

The good woman sighed as she saw him stride away to his fields. She would have liked her husband to agree with her on all points; but that is a bliss which is never granted to wives in this unsatisfactory world. So she prudently resolved that she would avoid discussing Nelly for the future; and we may be sure that she broke her resolution before it was many hours old.

CHAPTER XI.

DEADLY PERIL.

> "And hark, and hark! The deep-mouth'd bark
> Comes nigher still, and nigher."
> LAY OF THE LAST MINSTREL.

THE picnic was like any other picnic; the party strolled through the woods; they ascended the downs; they gathered prodigious handfuls of wild flowers and grasses. Some of the younger girls really enjoyed themselves, being at that happy age when cloudless skies, golden sunshine, and an excellent lunch on the grass, are all that is necessary for supreme happiness. But Nelly was distinctly bored.

Christina's guests were not many, and the men were uninteresting. Nelly did not care about the admiration of the curate and the village doctor; and it was impossible not to feel that Christina detested her. Phyllis was merry; but Mayne and Susie would rather have been at home.

It was Christina who decreed that the men should have a quiet half hour after lunch, and be left to smoke in peace. Amongst them was a rich bachelor cousin of hers, a man past fifty, whose favour she was anxious to win. Detecting the signs of incipient fatigue in his face, she announced that she was going to lead off a band of the younger ladies as an exploring party. The matrons were to remain behind, and the gentlemen were expressly forbidden to follow. The girls were to roam about until they had found a suitable spot for a gipsy tea. Then they were to return to the luncheon-ground, and invite their lovers, brothers, and admirers to join them again.

As to the men, they made but a very faint protest against this arrangement. The bachelor

cousin was delighted; he had got into a cosy
nook under a tree, and after a hearty yawn
he stretched himself out on the grass and fell
asleep. The curate, propping his back against
the trunk of an oak, indulged in a dreamy
doze; and Mayne, feeling curiously tired and
depressed, turned his back on his companions
and wondered why he wasn't enjoying himself.

Nelly had been behaving beautifully all the
morning. Her meek devotion to her betrothed
had exasperated Christina, and stirred up a mild
envy in the curate's placid breast. She had
been so lovely and gentle and dutiful that
Mayne could find no fault in her at all. And
yet here he was, supporting himself on his
elbow and plucking up little tufts of grass, with
a miserable consciousness that he was not a
perfectly happy man.

He had had a bad night, to begin with.
After lying awake for hours, listening to the
familiar creaking of the old furniture, and the

nibbling of mice behind the wainscot, he had dropped asleep to dream hideously.

It was as evil a vision as that which came to Sir Tristram in——

> "The lodge of intertwisted beechen-boughs
> Furze-crammed, and bracken-roof'd;"

and like his, it was a vision of rubies.

Mayne had dreamed that he saw Nelly, gay and radiant, with a necklace of large red gems clasping her white throat; and he was angry because these rubies were no gift of his. In his fury he tried to snatch them from her neck; but they would not come away, and then he saw that his hand was red.

And in a moment there had flashed into his mind the sickening words—

> "These be no rubies, this is frozen blood."

He had started up in bed with those words ringing in his ears, and found the broadening

day sending rays of light across the room. Here,
lying on the warm grass in the afternoon
sunshine, the dream came back with terrible
distinctness. He might rail at himself for being
a superstitious fool; but who does not know
what it is to have the spirit darkened by the
memory of an evil dream?

All around him the summer world was
steeped in rich repose. A humble-bee droned
close to his face, and then alighted near
enough for him to inspect its black velvet
coat belted with yellow. While he lay and
watched its movements, a drowsiness began to
steal over him; the bachelor cousin snored
under a neighbouring tree; but there was no
other sound to break the stillness of the place.
He slept; and this time his slumber was dream-
less and deep.

Christina's party gradually broke up into
twos and threes. A girl of seventeen attached
herself to Nelly, who did not want her in

the least, but was civil and sweet as usual.
Molly Dale, however, was not an exacting companion; she asked nothing more than to walk
by the side of this new beauty from London,
and be favoured with a commonplace remark
now and then. People and things were apt
to grow monotonous in Molly's everyday life;
but here was a bright creature from another
kind of world, arrived as unexpectedly as if
she were created to make a fresh delight in a
country holiday.

Nelly was in no mood to climb the downs
again. She showed a preference for quiet green
lanes, dark with the shadows of trees, where
the bindweed netted up the hedges, and black-
berries were ripening unseen. It was a sultry
afternoon; not a breath of wind stirred the
thick gold of the cornfields; scarcely a leaf
rustled overhead.

They had turned into a shady way which
appeared to lead to nowhere; weeds were

growing in old wheel tracks; the white flints
stood out in sharp relief against the grassy
ruts; no sound broke the silence that seemed
to reign here perpetually. It was a forsaken
way leading to a forgotten goal; a path that
might have depressed some travellers even in
broad sunshine.

"Don't you think we are rambling too far?"
asked Molly at last. "The others will be turning back to the luncheon-ground. And we
promised that we wouldn't go far, you know?"

"I didn't promise anything," Nelly answered.
"I want to see if this lane has an end."

Molly was too meek to offer a remonstrance.
She gave a thought to the handsome lover
who was awaiting Miss Stanley's return with
impatience, of course; but she did not venture
to remind her new acquaintance of his prob-
able anxiety. Nelly had not forgotten him;
to do her justice he was very seldom out of
her mind; but his depression had not escaped

her notice, and she had resented it a little. She had behaved well,—exceedingly well—all the day, and had made herself as unattractive as possible to the other men. Yet Mayne had not appeared to appreciate her goodness; it was all lost upon him, she thought.

Well, he might pay attention to Christina if he chose. She would give him an opportunity to be agreeable in that quarter. Mayne would miss her when they all reassembled; but every one knew that Molly Dale was her sole companion. They could not suspect her of stealing off with the curate, reflected Nelly with a smile.

"Here's the end at last," said Molly, in a tone of relief. She was getting tired of this silent walk, and half regretted forsaking Christina's party.

She was right. The lane terminated in a triangle from which the high hedges afforded only one outlet. A stile of the roughest description led into a beautiful field.

"How pretty!" Molly exclaimed. "That's Rosedown."

Beyond the field there was a long, low house, built on rising ground, a house with white walls and many windows. The girls could catch glimpses of terraces and gardens, just visible through breaks in the belt of woodland which divided Rosedown from the field.

"It belongs to Lord Rexbury," Molly went on; but Nelly was mounting the stile, and did not heed her.

"I am going to get a nearer view of the place," Miss Stanley said quietly. "Don't come; I'm sure you are tired, and I shall return in a few minutes."

Molly seated herself on the top rail, and watched the graceful figure moving away. Nelly was wearing her black lace hat laden with poppies, and had brightened a fawn-coloured gown with a full vest of soft scarlet silk. The rich colour showed out bravely against the background of green; the sun shone on the solitary form in its tasteful dress, and good-natured little Molly followed it with admiring eyes.

On one side of the field, not many yards from the spot where Molly sat waiting for her companion, there was a thicket, and a group of small oaks. The girl, absorbed in looking after Miss Stanley, enjoyed the quietness of her shady seat, and vaguely realized that she was just fatigued enough to feel the pleasantness of rest. Suddenly a deep bellow, fierce and thunderous, startled her out of her musings, and drew from her an involuntary scream of terror. A bull, which had been screened by the thicket, was advancing slowly out into the open ground.

Molly, in the suddenness of her fright, fell backwards from her seat on the rail, and fortunately slipped into a dry ditch under the hedge, doing herself little harm. She was safe,

at any rate; the high stile and higher hedge
were between her and the bull; and for a few
moments she crouched trembling in the mossy
trench into which she had fallen. Then she
rose, still quaking in every limb, and looked
through the bars into the field.

Alas for Nelly, and the bravery of her scarlet
adorning! The bull was following her with venge-
ful purpose, still moving deliberately, and
pawing the sod now and then. She had looked
back and seen her pursuer; but her presence
of mind had not deserted her yet, and she was
walking swiftly, but without any appearance of
undue haste.

"Don't run!" shrieked Molly at the top of
her voice.

Another bellow, louder and more threaten-
ing, came from the angry brute, who was
evidently quickening his pace. He was a fine
fellow, with a pale tawny hide, and horns as
black as jet, descended from an ancient race

which had once roamed in the forests of the north in all the pride of strength and freedom. That last roar of his was too much for Nelly. Her self-possession broke down all at once, and she set off running as fast as her light feet would go.

The bull pursued her at the top of his speed. Molly, half mad with horror and agony, climbed the stile again, and filled the air with screams for aid. The frantic chase went on as if it would never end. Nelly was a fleet runner; but the day was warm, she had already done a great deal of walking, and was tired. At first, fear had lent her speed; but the pace was too good to last; once or twice she stumbled; there was a singing in her ears; a mist before her eyes.

Even to the wildly-excited Molly it was clear that the bull was gaining on his victim. Poor Nelly's strength was fast ebbing away; field and trees and sky seemed to be whirling round and round her as she ran. In a vague way she was making for the thick belt of woodland which lay between the field and the grounds of Rosedown; a small white gate gleamed before her dim eyes,—if it could be reached she might make a desperate effort to climb it and be safe. But could she reach it? O for one moment of rest!

On, on, although her senses seemed to be forsaking her, and the whole thing began to grow like a hideous nightmare. Her foot struck against a mole-hill; she half fell, recovered herself, and staggered along, more slowly now. In a second or two she felt that she should fall again.

There was another bellow behind her, terribly close this time. And then came the deep, strong bark of a dog; then more bellowing, and a great uproar of barking and roaring. The white gate was near—nearer than she had thought. If she could but gain a little breathing-time she might be saved yet.

The uproar in the rear continued; but it sounded farther off. In sheer desperation Nelly paused and looked behind.

What she saw was a fierce conflict going on between the bull and two huge mastiffs. The dogs harassed him on the right and left, turning him now this way, and now that. Panting fearfully, still half despairing of escape, the girl tried to run on again, and dragged herself along a little way. She was close to the gate now, so close that in another moment she might have touched it. But sight and sense failed; she stumbled once more, and then seemed to plunge downward into a world of darkness.

Molly, on the top of the stile, had screamed until her voice was gone, and now stood babbling incoherent words of trouble. She could see it all from her standpoint; the attack of the dogs; the fury of the thwarted bull; poor Nelly's headlong fall.

Would the mastiffs succeed in keeping the
bull away from the helpless heap, lying close
to the little white gate? That perfect form,
those peach-tinted cheeks, set in masses of
warm brown hair, all the charms which men's
eyes had loved to dwell upon! What would
they be presently? O brave dogs, keep the
cruel brute at bay! Give him not a moment's
peace, good dogs, harry him, vex him, tire
him out!

A flash; a sharp report from the wood; and
the furious animal tumbled forward on his knees.
In the next instant he was rolling on the ground
in the last convulsions of the death struggle;
and Molly saw a couple of men emerging from
the shade of the trees with guns in their hands.

Terrified as she still was, Molly Dale summoned strength enough to get over the stile,
and run across the field to the place where
Nelly lay. But long before she reached the
spot, one of the men had lifted the girl gently

from the ground, and was doing his best to bring her back to consciousness when her companion came up.

CHAPTER XII.

ROSEDOWN.

"What sort of a world will the world be now?
Oh, never again what the world hath been!
And how happened the marvellous change?"
OWEN MEREDITH.

"I WILL carry her into the house," said Lord Wyburn. These were the first words that Nelly heard when her senses were coming slowly back. She did not know the voice, nor could she tell in whose arms she lay. But a look of relief came into her languid eyes when she recognized Molly Dale's face bending over her.

"Don't be frightened, dear," entreated Molly,

whose country cheeks were as white as ashes. "It's all over now, you know; you are quite safe."

"The bull?" gasped poor Nelly faintly.

"He'll never trouble anybody again," said the voice which had first spoken. "I've put a bullet into him, and he's quiet enough now."

Molly remembered afterwards that Lord Wyburn had been in no haste to relinquish his burden. He was looking down into the lovely face, and watching the life-tints stealing back into lips and cheeks, with an intense, passionate gaze which startled even the simple Molly.

"Can you walk, Nelly?" she faltered out timidly.

"Of course she cannot." Lord Wyburn answered for her. "It would be dangerous to try her strength yet. I shall carry her into the house, and send a servant to her people."

"But—I can walk," Nelly feebly protested.

"Not to be thought of. Your friend will

come with you, and you'll be quite well presently. If you fight against your weakness you'll make yourself awfully ill," said the young man, in a stern tone of warning.

Nelly was far too much exhausted to protest any more. The keeper, who stood by, opened the gate which led into the wood; and Lord Wyburn lifted her up as lightly as if she had been a child. He was rather below middle height, but his broad shoulders and strong arms could have sustained a heavier weight with ease.

The girl, with eyes closed, and long black lashes lying on her pale cheeks, felt that she was being carried with infinite tenderness. Very slowly he moved along the path which cut right through the little wood; and presently a wave of rich perfume from the flower-gardens swept over her. They were entering the shrubberies of Rosedown.

She opened her eyes upon a paradise of

flowers. There were old fish-ponds with swans, and tall reeds, and floating water-plants; a fountain, its basin garlanded with the luxuriant leaves and blossoms of a purple creeper, flashed and tinkled in the sunshine. Close by, a Psyche lifted her pure face heavenward, her marble limbs gleaming out of a drapery of pendant foliage. About the whole place there lingered an antique charm; it was a bit of dreamland, sheltered from the innovating hands of the age, and wrapped in drowsy peace.

Lord Wyburn walked on in silence with his burden. Molly, still in a dazed condition, followed meekly, carrying the black lace hat trimmed with poppies. Nelly's soft hair had come unbound, and hung in a mass of ripples over Lord Wyburn's arm. She drew a long breath now and then, but neither spoke nor moved.

He carried her gently up the broad stone steps of the terrace, through a portico, into a

dim hall, and on into a long, low room. Still
with the same care and tenderness he placed
her on a large, easy couch which stood near
one of the windows, and then withdrew, leaving
her with Molly alone.

Lying there, in the quietness of utter pros-
tration, Nelly gazed around her with dreamy
eyes, and saw pictures, and statuettes, and a
great quantity of old china. There were four
windows, looking out upon the terrace, and
myrtle and roses clustered round them in rich
profusion. Beyond the silent gardens, the marble figures, the fountains, and fish-ponds,
stretched the billowy country with its cornfields
and pasture-lands all steeped in golden sunshine.
Farther away against the horizon rose the grey
towers of Abbeyside, crowning a low hill, and
looking down upon the dark woods that came
half way up the height.

" Nelly—Miss Stanley—" said Molly, coming
up to the couch, and speaking in a frightened

whisper, "do you think you are going to be very ill?"

Nelly roused herself, and smiled for the first time since her terrible adventure.

"No," she answered. "I think you are more likely to be ill than I am, you poor child! I couldn't have believed that your rosy cheeks could get so pale. I brought all this trouble on myself, you know," she added in a penitent tone.

"No, you didn't," Molly declared. "That beastly bull ought to have been shot long ago. But oh, what will Mayne Comberford say to this business?"

What would he say? Nelly's heart began to throb very fast at the mention of his name. She sank back on the cushions with a heavy sigh, feeling that she would have given anything she possessed if his arms could have carried her out of danger. That Lord Wyburn, of all men, should have been singled out by fate to be her preserver, was a disastrous thing indeed!

"Mayne will never forgive him," she thought. "And I shall never make him understand that I hated the man's touch, and wanted my own lover all the while. Mayne will look at me with his beautiful, reproachful blue eyes, and I shall feel as if I had enticed the bull to run after me on purpose to get rescued by Lord Wyburn. Dear Mayne, he has such a talent for putting one in the wrong! But I wish—oh, how I wish that I could see him at this moment! Molly!"

"Yes, dear; I am here."

"Yes, you are there, but you are not of much use. Oh, poor child, I don't mean to be cross, but I am feeling intensely miserable. This is such a silent, mysterious place that it frightens me! Are they never coming? Look out of the window, Molly, and tell me if you can see anything of Mayne."

Nelly was beginning to cry. She lay on

the sofa with a lovely, distressed face that looked like a child's. Two ladies, who entered the room together, were struck by this half-babyish expression of woe; and one of them was conscious of a sharp thrill of sad remembrance. In the years gone by (more years than she cared to count), she had seen a child's face wear that selfsame look.

The elder lady, who was tall, strong, and handsome in a hard, patrician style, came over to the sofa. She began to speak to the girl in a kindly, business-like fashion.

"Don't cry, my dear; you must drink this at once," she said, taking some wine from a servant, and administering it to Nelly with her own hands.

The other lady, who was much younger, advanced with a graceful step, and stood looking down at the unexpected guest with eyes that were darker and deeper than her own.

Nelly, who had been on the verge of a fit

of hysterical weeping, made a desperate struggle
to regain her self-control.   She drank the wine,
murmured a grateful word or two to Lady
Rexbury (who shook up the sofa-pillows and
told her to lie still); and sank back obediently
into the satiny nest.

"Let me sit with her," said a voice, low
and harmonious by nature.   "You are wanted
elsewhere, and she is getting better already."

It was the dark-eyed lady who spoke; and
Nelly looked at her face with a vague remembrance of having seen it before.

"Her portrait must have been in the Royal
Academy," she thought.   "It is just the kind
of face to delight a painter."

It was, indeed, the kind of face which smiles
down upon you from the walls of picture-
galleries; dark, richly beautiful, possessing a
strange witchery of expression which arrests
the gaze at once.   Something picturesque and
foreign lingered about this woman, and dis-

tinguished her from others, although her dress was as perfectly correct as it is possible for a faultlessly-made costume to be. Her features, small and regular, were of the Greek type; but the eyes had a latent fire in their darkness; they were eyes that seemed to speak of passion and remembrance.

Lady Brookstone was past thirty, but her lustrous black hair showed no thread of silver. It was coiled about her small head in massive braids in a fashion which is never out of date, and drawn back simply from her low, broad forehead. Her skin was of a dark clear brunette hue, with a rich red in the cheeks and lips. She had the art of choosing the colours which suited her best, and was wearing a soft gown of some deep cream-coloured stuff, trimmed sparingly with amber silk and black lace.

She sat down in a chair by the couch, and presently her small fingers wandered over Nelly's brow, among the little curls and rings of brown hair.

Molly Dale, whose presence had been smil-ingly acknowledged by Lady Rexbury, sat in silence on a lounge near the window, and watched "the dark ladye" with a fascinated gaze.

The gentle movements went on without ceasing; the lady's intense dark eyes were bent unwaveringly upon the lovely face on the sofa pillows. There was a golden stillness in the gardens; rich odours floated into the room; not a sound was to be heard in the house; and Molly found a pleasant drowsiness stealing over her as she sat in her cushioned seat. Just as she was sinking into a tranquil doze her glance was attracted towards something that moved in the doorway; and she saw Lord Wyburn standing there.

Without noticing her in the least, he walked noiselessly into the room, and stood by Lady Brookstone's side, looking down intently on the sleeping girl. Molly, now thoroughly aroused saw a sort of white light pass across his face. His eyes shone; he drew a step nearer to the sleeper; and Lady Brookstone laid her hand gently on his arm.

"Hush," she whispered.

The touch seemed to recall him to himself. After standing there perfectly motionless for a moment or two, he allowed the lady to push him quietly away. He even smiled at her for doing so; and the smile improved his face.

His retreating footsteps made no sound upon the soft carpet. He departed as silently as he had come.

CHAPTER XIII.

CHATTERING.

The small, small imperceptible
  Small talk, that cuts like powdered glass
Ground in Tophana,—who can tell
  Where lurks the power the poison has?
                                OWEN MEREDITH.

"WASN'T it strange," said Phyllis, "that such a dull picnic should have had such a romantic ending?"

A family group had assembled under the great cedar on the lawn. It was Saturday afternoon; Nelly, still weak and languid after yesterday's adventure, was lying down in her own room upstairs. Mayne, his face unusually pale and worn, sat on the grass by his mother's side. His sisters were talking over the eventful day with Molly Dale.

"It was a dull picnic," Susie admitted. "We all felt so stupid that no ordinary occurrence could have roused us. Even when we had gone back to the luncheon-ground, and Nelly and Molly were missing, we——"

"Oh, but we were not kept long in suspense," Phyllis broke · in. "The man-servant from Rosedown appeared, and told his little story beautifully. It was rather mean of you and Mayne to start off to Nelly without me. I wanted to see the house."

"It is not so old as ours," said Mrs. Comberford. "There is nothing remarkable about it."

"The grounds are charming," Molly remarked. "Perhaps I was fanciful, but it seemed to me that I must have read about Rosedown in some old romance. And that dark lady who sent Nelly to sleep;—she was a kind of enchantress."

"My dear Molly, I think you were over-excited," Mrs. Comberford said, glancing up from her work.

"I dare say I was." Molly seldom contradicted anybody. "But she did put Nelly to sleep, you know, and it was the best thing that could have been done; Nelly woke refreshed and rested. There's something very uncommon in Lady Brookstone."

"Your fancy must have coloured everything and every one, Molly," Mrs. Comberford answered.

"I don't think Molly has coloured things as much as you suppose, mother," said Susie quietly. "Lady Brookstone is exactly like some one in a poem or a play. Yes," added the girl, looking away across the lawn with dreamy eyes, "she is like the gipsy mother in Il Trovatore. I can imagine her in a gay costume, glittering with golden coins, singing those wonderful, passionate songs."

"I believe you are all a little mad to-day," observed Mrs. Comberford, in a grant-me-patience tone. "I shall be glad when you have forgotten this interesting affair altogether. It was very wicked of Lord Rexbury to keep such a horrible bull in his field."

" But Lord Wyburn behaved well, didn't he?" Molly said timidly. "And he was anxious — oh, very anxious about poor Nelly. He picked her up from the ground, and carried her into the house—carried her in his arms as tenderly as you would hold a baby! And when she was asleep on the couch, he came and looked at her so earnestly that Lady Brookstone had to send him away."

Mrs. Comberford felt rather than saw Mayne's start. At that moment this good matron was unreasonably angry with two or three people at once. She longed to box the ears of the innocent narrator of the story; she would have liked to rate Nelly soundly for letting herself be carried by that titled *roué*, whose admiration, she thought, was an insult; and she was vexed with her own dear boy for his unfortunate infatuation.

There are times in every mother's life when she longs to play the part of providence, and "change this sorry scheme of things entire." In fact, if she spoke out of the depths of her heart she would say that she ought to be providence to her children. How wisely she would direct their affections if they would but consent to be guided! What troubles and mistakes they might be spared if they would but submit to her rule!

Poor Molly's last words were succeeded by a profound silence. The amiable blunderer opened her round grey eyes, and looked at them all with an inquiring gaze.

"Here is Christina," exclaimed Phyllis, getting up from her seat on the grass, and going to meet Miss Payton.

Christina came in among them all with sympathetic smiles, and kind inquiries. They gave her a cane chair under the cedar; and then the event of yesterday had to be discussed again.

"It's like the beginning of a novel, isn't it!" said Phyllis. "That's how Ravenswood and Lucy Ashton fell in love, you remember? He shot the bull just as she sank exhausted to the ground."

"Oh, we must hope that it's not the beginning of such a tragedy as the Bride of Lammermoor," cried Christina, in a shocked tone. "I am sure poor Miss Stanley must have suffered very much," she added smoothly. "Lord Wyburn had to carry her to the house, I am told. So unpleasant for her, was it not? I really don't think I could have borne it."

"I could," said Phyllis. "I can't think why things always happen to other girls and never to me. I should like immensely to faint, and be carried out of danger in the arms of a nobleman."

"Phyllis, if you talk such nonsense I shall send you to your room," said Mrs. Comberford severely.

"It was unpleasant; very unpleasant," Christina repeated. "We will trust that the whole thing will soon be done with, and forgotten. But such sensational adventures are remembered for a long time, especially in the country. I don't believe in a nine days' wonder. All the wonders I have ever known have lasted much longer than nine days."

Just then Nelly herself came slowly out of the shade of the porch, and moved towards the group with the languid step of weakness. Her cheeks wore a clear pallor which gave her a new aspect, and made her eyebrows and lashes look blacker than ever. Mayne sprang up, and hastened to her side; but she saw the shadow on his face.

He waited upon her with loving care, bringing her tea and cake. Susie hovered round her with gentle little attentions; Phyllis was frankly affectionate, and Mrs. Comberford kind. Yet Nelly's heart was ill at ease; she knew that her lover suffered; she felt that there were thorns already among love's roses. Alas! it was so early to find the thorns.

Christina took her leave, and Mrs. Comberford accompanied her down the carriage-drive. The poor mother was longing for sympathy; it was a relief to speak her thoughts to a friend.

"My children are all absurdly romantic," she said. "They don't take it from their father or me. It must have come from their Aunt Adeliza, who played the guitar, and tried to live in accordance with her ridiculous name. If it hadn't been for poor Angela's romantic school-friendship we should never have known Nelly."

"I hope you are not disappointed in Miss Stanley," said Christina, in a tone of concern.

"Not exactly disappointed. She is very charming, of course. But it grieves me to see my boy so completely enthralled. It is not a restful, satisfying love; it makes him jealous and unhappy."

"She may, perhaps, be a *little* too fond of admiration," murmured Christina softly. "The idea occurred to me when I saw her first."

"I am afraid you are right," Mrs. Comberford replied. They were standing at the gate, and both looked up at the sound of approaching wheels.

"Here is a carriage from Abbeyside," Christina exclaimed. "Some of the family are coming to make inquiries."

Mrs. Comberford's face flushed with annoyance. "I hope Lord Wyburn hasn't come," she said; and then turned back to the house.

Lord Wyburn had come, and Lady Brookstone had accompanied him. They joined the group under the cedar; and there were pleasant words, soft laughter, and inward heartburnings.

Wyburn made several attempts to begin a

quiet conversation with Nelly, but was foiled by Mayne with courtesy and skill. The two young men were but slightly acquainted; there had never been any intimacy between Abbeyside and the manor. The earl and countess seldom entertained their neighbours; they had people down from London after the season, and kept their house full till the shooting was over. The countess did not like Abbeyside well enough to stay there very long; she always said it was necessary for the earl to go abroad a good deal; so abroad they went. The old place on the hill was shut up during the greater part of the year.

Lady Brookstone sat down by Nelly's side, and looked earnestly into the girl's face, pale and weary, but beautiful beyond compare.

"I am glad I chanced to be at Rosedown yesterday," she said. "The house is to be refurnished, and Lady Rexbury had asked me to go there with her. We were looking over

things when Lord Wyburn brought you in.
What a dreadful affair it was, poor child!"

"I have quite got over it," said Nelly.

"I don't think you have." Lady Brookstone
regarded her with a doubtful glance.

"But I have, indeed. I am very strong. I
mustn't forget to thank you for soothing me to
sleep; it was a delicious rest."

"Did you know that I soothed you to sleep?
The process was very simple," said Lady
Brookstone smiling. "Some can do it, and
some cannot. I have often lulled my children
in the same way."

"You have children?" Nelly looked up with
bright interest at "the dark ladye."

"Yes, I have two boys. But no girl; and
I have always wanted a daughter."

The visitors departed. Mayne led Nelly
away, later on, to see the sunset from the
rising ground behind the house. She was still
weary, and leaned on his arm for support.

" Dear," he said, "I have been trying to keep my temper; but you know I hate the sight of that fellow. It's too bad that *he* should have saved your life?"

"It was a great deal too bad," she answered. "I wish it had been any one else. Let us forget all about it, Mayne. If you like, I will promise never to go to another picnic as long as I live. I won't go to any more parties given by Miss Payton, I assure you. She is my pet aversion."

CHAPTER XIV.

WITH THE CAMDENS AGAIN.

The little rift within the lover's lute,
That by and by will make the music mute,
And ever widening slowly silence all.

TENNYSON.

IN the country, as Christina had said, a wonder lasts longer than nine days. The country

people enjoyed Nelly's adventure so much that
they could not have enough of it. It was discussed

"At kirk and at market;"

in the village street; in every lane and corner
of Hartside. That the vicar's daughter did
her best to keep the matter before the public,
goes without saying. Any one who desired to
obtain full particulars was sure of getting ample
information at the vicarage.

The farmers' wives were sorry for poor Mr.
Mayne, who had gone up to London, and got
bewitched by a flirting young woman. The
Comberfords, it was remarked, had trouble
enough already; why did Mr. Mayne bring
home a stranger to disturb the peace of the
family? Why not have set his heart on some
good girl well known in the neighbourhood,
—somebody like Miss Payton, for instance?
As to beauty,—well, in a year or two one
woman would be as good-looking as another.

Susie was a wise girl; but with all her wisdom she could not succeed in controlling the active tongue of Phyllis. Both the sisters were deeply interested in her whom they called "the dark ladye," and they had discovered a resemblance between her and Nelly. When told of this discovery Nelly had admitted that Lady Brookstone had reminded her of some one; but it had not occurred to her that the "some one" was herself. Phyllis, delighted with the likeness, chattered about it continually. Mayne obstinately denied that it existed at all.

Yet it did exist, although Lady Brookstone was two or three shades darker than Nelly. The features of the two were dissimilar; but there were looks, smiles, a quick lighting-up of the two faces which made them alike.

"I don't want Lady Brookstone to come here again," said Mayne impatiently. "She is too soft and cooing for my taste; I distrust women of that type. And she belongs to the Rexbury set."

To belong to the Rexbury set was to lose all chance of finding favour in Mayne's sight.

Nelly's holiday was slipping fast away; and as it drew near its close she confessed to herself that it had not been a time of unalloyed pleasure. It had begun with disappointment; it ended with a cloud of doubt and depression.

It was good to be going back to the life that she had lived in Russell Square—good to think of Robby's welcoming eyes, and Louie's smile, and Lady Florence's cordial greeting. Her mind went back to her first meeting with Mayne on the quiet Sunday morning in Lincoln's Inn. It was only a girlish fancy, but it seemed as if there was a sweet spell in that old place. Memories of ancient loves lingered about it like the scent of dried roses. The musty atmosphere of the law was sweetened by that delicate, yet unconquerable fragrance of the past.

"When I go back again I shall get on better

with Mayne," she thought. "He will forget his jealousy, and his mother and Christina will not be at hand with their irritating speeches. A pair of lovers ought to have a little world all to themselves. We shall find our little world in Lincoln's Inn, and the stranger shall not intermeddle with our joy."

Lady Florence wrote to tell Nelly to join her pupils at Sandown. After a month with them at Eastbourne Aunt Margery had had quite enough of their society. All Lady Florence's predictions had been fulfilled; Miss Camden had boxed the ears of Robby the Roarer, and Robby had soundly belaboured her in return.

"It served her right," Nelly murmured. "Dear little man—how glad I shall be to hear him stutter again!"

She said good-bye to the manor on the first of September. It was a soft, rain-scented morning; the first breath of autumn came sighing over the hills; a few russet leaves had drifted across the lawn. Mayne had arranged to travel with his betrothed as far as Portsmouth, and then to go on to London.

They had taken an early breakfast, and the old fly waited at the door. The father and mother and the two girls came out with them to the porch with kisses and farewells. At this last moment all were a little sad. Nelly was grave and sweet; something in her face touched Mrs. Comberford, bringing unexpected tears into her eyes.

"Good-bye, my dear," she said, with more warmth than she had ever shown before. "You must come to us again very soon."

The fly rolled away, down the carriage-drive and through the gates; but Nelly only looked back once to the group standing in the porch. The fragrance of showers, and the odour of the pines came to her, blending with the strange sadness of that leave-taking. Far off, the pale blue of the horizon was dim with thin veils of rain.

"You are very quiet, Nelly," said Mayne, taking her hand. "Are you sorry that your holiday is over?"

"It is not over yet," she answered. "The children will have no lessons to learn at Sandown."

"I shall not be with you at Sandown," he said, looking deep into her brown eyes.

"But you will meet me in London. Oh, Mayne, it will be good to see old Lincoln's Inn again! Somehow the place seems to belong to us; it has been our meeting-place, and we have made it our own."

He bent over her tenderly.

"You are right," he said. "We have made it our own."

A few hours later Nelly and her luggage arrived at the seaside villa, where the Camdens were finishing their summer holiday. Robby, radiant and rosy, was the first to give her a hug and a greeting.

"Oh, what a long time, what a long time!" began the boy. "I—I—I—s—said I wouldn't st—st—stutter when I saw you."

"He is not to be allowed to kiss you till to-morrow morning if he stutters," said Lady Florence. "But, Nelly, you are looking rather pale. What has taken your roses away?"

"Aunt Margery g—g—gave it to me," shouted Robby, following his governess upstairs. "And I g—g—gave it to her back again!"

Alone in a pretty bed-room overlooking the sea, Nelly shed a few tears that night. She missed Mayne; but there was a sense of relief in getting back to Robby and Louie; and she cried, in true girlish fashion, because she was glad to find herself with the children again.

It was so easy to please the Camdens, she thought. The barrister and Lady Florence approved of all that she did; her pupils wel-

comed her with unfeigned delight. She recalled Mrs. Comberford's look of cold doubt,
and felt that it was pleasant to escape from
those unloving eyes. Mayne—dear Mayne—
was her true love; but she loved him better
under the historic trees of Lincoln's Inn than
in the beautiful old home of his boyhood.
People in love may well be forgiven for regret-
ting, like the little American girl, that "the
world is so full of other people." It is seldom,
indeed, that "other people" do anything to
help the course of that sweet passion which
"never did run smooth."

Next day Lady Florence conducted the
governess to a nook on the sands, and sent
the children away to collect shells and sea-
weed. Louie, who showed an inclination to
linger within earshot, was promptly provided
with a basket, and reminded of the marine
album which would be the reward of her
industry. The album was to have scarlet

covers lettered with the initials !.. C. Uncle Giffard had promised a sea-sketch for the first page.

Lady Florence was one of the many childless women who can manage children beautifully. Tactless mothers envied her skill; aggrieved little ones turned instinctively to her for sympathy. When persuasion could prevail she never commanded; Nelly smiled as she saw Louie take herself off with a well-pleased face.

"And now," began Lady Florence, turning to her young companion, "I want to hear the history of your holiday from beginning to end."

"But I'm afraid it won't be interesting," said Nelly, with a blush.

"The holiday of a pretty girl is never devoid of interest. Understand that I will not let you leave out all the thrilling parts. Tell me everything."

Nelly's blush deepened.

"Shall I begin your story for you?" Lady Florence asked mischievously. "You are engaged to Mr. Mayne Comberford."

"How did you know?" said Nelly, opening her brown eyes.

"By this." Lady Florence lightly touched the ruby ring on the girl's hand.

Nelly had grown accustomed to the ring, and had quite forgotten that it was likely to attract notice.

"It is true," she admitted after a pause. "But, Lady Florence, it will be such a long engagement that I see no good in proclaiming it to the world."

"I do not like long engagements as a rule. However, you are young enough to wait a year or two. Now, Nelly, I have made the beginning; you must go on with the story."

And Nelly obeyed. As she went on she began to enjoy the interest she excited; Lady Florence listened with unusual animation.

"You must tell it all over again to my husband, Nelly," she exclaimed. "He will thoroughly enjoy the bull-fight! You want to know if I have ever met Lady Brookstone? Yes; she is one of those women who might be a professional beauty if she cared for that kind of celebrity."

"Then she doesn't care?" said Nelly.

"Not in the least. She was married to her husband in his old Bohemian days. Lord Brookstone used to be plain Leonard Hilton, a poor artist, earning his bread from the illustrated papers. One or two unexpected deaths gave him the barony; but some say that he looks back with regret to the old roving life. I don't know who his wife was. Nobody makes any inquiries about her antece-dents; she is beautiful and refined, and a general favourite. But she does not care to attract much notice, and is quite devoted to her husband."

"And is he devoted to her?" Nelly asked.

"Entirely. In short, they are a model couple. You admired her, of course; she is as good to look at as a picture. She makes one think of lotus flowers and the Nile."

"I should like to meet her again," said Nelly, in a thoughtful tone. "She asked where my home was, and I said that I lived with you."

"Then it is possible that she will come to see you, child. After your adventure, it is natural that she should wish to know how you get on."

There was a look of hesitation and doubt on the girl's face, and Lady Florence perceived it.

"Don't you really want her to come, Nelly?" she asked.

"I should like to see her again. But—Mayne does not want me to get better acquainted with her."

"Why not? There is nothing that can be said against the Brookstones."

"He has taken a dislike to her, I am afraid."

"I hope he is not a man who takes dislikes,"
Lady Florence remarked. "If he is, he'll be
difficult to live with. What has Lady Brookstone done to offend him?"

"Nothing. He dislikes her because she is
in the Rexbury set; that is all."

Lady Florence sat still and mused, looking
out across the blue water in silence.

"I see," she said at last. "He is furiously
jealous of Lord Wyburn."

"It is so," Nelly answered in a resigned
voice.

"'The little rift within the lover's lute',"
Lady Florence murmured. "Don't let him
become a tyrant, Nelly. If you do not stand
up for yourself now, it will be too late by-
and-by."

CHAPTER XV.

"THE DARK LADYE."

Rose-bloom fell on her hands together prest,
    And on her silver cross soft amethyst,
And on her hair a glory like a saint:
    She seemed a splendid angel, newly drest
Save wings, for heaven.

KEATS.

OCTOBER had come; there were golden sunsets veiled in the mists of London; russet leaves drifted about the quiet precincts of Lincoln's Inn; the last flowers of summer withered slowly in the barristers' quaint little gardens. On Sundays the chapel was open again; Nelly and the children went back to their old pew in the chancel, and Mayne became a regular worshipper there.

It is not for us to seek to analyse that wor-

ship. There is something divine in the first
true love of a young man for a young woman;
and it has been finely said that "the power of
love in all ages creates angels." Nelly, standing quietly in her place in the old chapel,
never knew how deep a reverence blended
with her lover's devotion.

He had grown intimately acquainted with
all the saints in the gorgeous old windows, and
knew what rich depths of colour lurked in
those ample folds of purple and crimson and
violet which draped them with such regal
splendour. The preacher, with his tall, slight
figure, and clean-cut scholarly face, had the
look of an abbot of the Middle Ages; and
Mayne liked him. He even liked the imperious,
old bidding prayer which commanded him to
pray "especially for this learned and honourable
Society." In those days, when he had come
out of a noisy world into the shade and quietness of this sanctuary, it seemed an easy thing

to be in charity with all men. The mysterious
light streamed through the painted glass on
Nelly's face, and his soul was at peace. Every-
one, who is worth anything, has a romance in
his own heart; and Mayne's was the Romance
of Lincoln's Inn.

That longing for steadfast tranquillity, which
Wordsworth believed to be one of the deepest
instincts of our nature, was almost satisfied in
Mayne's life just then. He saw Nelly often
on week-days, and met her always on Sundays.
Nothing was said or done that could disturb
his trust in her. Together they discussed their
plans for the future, and pictured that quiet
little home which was to be theirs one day.

In their Sunday walks they found out a
great many modest residences which would suit
them exactly, and even went so far as to fur-
nish them in imagination. We all know such
houses; they stand here and there in odd nooks
and corners of the great West-central district,

and are generally to be seen where there are a few trees, and a fragment of garden. They are the very dwellings for young couples of moderate means and simple tastes to settle in. And sometimes, a few of us who are dreamers can forget this weary world and all its dull necessities, in picturing simple lives of wedded love that might be lived within those walls.

"If we could only make a nest, as the birds do," said Nelly, one day, "how simple life would be! You would come with sticks and straws, and I should contribute bits of moss, and little morsels of down and wool. I know I should love to live in it after it was finished. Shouldn't you?"

"Very much," answered Mayne. "And I should like to perch it up on one of the topmost boughs in Lincoln's Inn, and get a bird's view of London. When I flew down to my daily work (I should want a pair of wings, you know), you might be busy with repairs. Every windy night would blow away little pieces of our home, so that there would be enough to do."

"I would execute all repairs myself," Nelly cried. "I shouldn't need any plumbers and glaziers, and drain-men, and gas-men, and all the horrid crew that come to a house, and make one's life a burden. The only difficulty would be the trifling one of food."

He looked smilingly into her eyes, and wondered what better thing could happen to a young man than that he should fall in love? The October afternoon was warm with mellow sunshine as they turned into Russell Square, and the light fell on the two bright young faces.

An old doctor, fat, but romantic, glanced kindly at them as he stepped out of his carriage, and recalled the experiences of his own youth with a sigh.

Afterwards, Mayne used to look back to that Sunday as the last day of rest. In most lives

there is a time of restfulness which precedes
the time of strife.   There is the golden dream
before the rude awaking ; the sweet communion
before the anguish of parting · the quiet sojourn
in that Land of Beulah which lies so close to
the brink of the mysterious River.   Who does
not remember the charm of those last hours?
Who does not know the mystic beauty of that
border country which comes between us and
the Unseen?

Lady Florence was kind to the lovers, and
Mayne sat down to the home-like tea-table in
the breakfast-room with Nelly and the children.

Robby, having been assured that he was
not to be parted from his governess until at
least half a century had expired, had struck up
a warm friendship with Mr. Comberford. Louie
thought Miss Stanley's friend was a decided
acquisition, and put on all sorts of little airs
and graces for his benefit.   Nelly, pouring out
tea, and smiling at the children's talk, had a

bewitching, matronly look which filled Mayne's cup of happiness to the brim.

Monday came, bringing the usual tasks to be gone through; but it brought something more than work. Returning from her afternoon walk with her pupils, Nelly was sent for by Lady Florence, and found Lady Brookstone in the drawing-room.

"You have quite recovered? Yes; I am sure of it," said "the dark ladye," taking the girl's hand affectionately.

In Nelly's sight she seemed handsomer than ever, that day. Her eyes were shining; her brown cheeks were touched with a deeper flush; there was a suppressed emotion in her manner. She held the little hand in a lingering clasp.

"I am perfectly well," Nelly answered. "And I am glad to come back to Russell Square. My adventure almost spoiled the visit to Hartside."

"I cannot think of it without a shudder," Lady Brookstone declared. "You were looking very pale when I saw you at the manor. Lord Wyburn has never ceased to talk about you; he showed a great deal of real feeling and anxiety."

"You were all most kind," murmured Nelly, conscious that she was blushing, and that Lady Florence was observing her narrowly.

"You must come and see us. We have come up to town for a fortnight, and then we go to Rome for the winter. Ah, how I wish I could take you with me!" said "the dark ladye" with the shining eyes.

Nelly was surprised, and a little embarrassed. Lady Brookstone departed after receiving a promise that Miss Stanley should go to her on Wednesday afternoon; and Lady Florence and the governess were left alone.

"Why does she want me?" asked the girl, with a puzzled look.

"Well, partly for the sake of your face, child," Lady Florence replied. "And there is another reason. She has heard the story of the little child who was found sitting by the roadside."

Nelly coloured with annoyance.

"I think Mrs. Comberford might have refrained from telling my story to all her neighbours!" she exclaimed. "I know she disapproves of her son's engagement; I know she will never like me; but——"

"You are not certain that she has talked about you, my dear. No one ever knows how news is circulated in the country. But Lady Brookstone, poor woman, has a sorrow of her own; and that is why she is so much interested in you. As I have told you, the early days of her married life were roving days; and it seems that she lost her first child—a little daughter. Her husband's wealth and title have never consoled her for that loss. Even her two boys cannot make her forget the sister they never knew. And she has taken it into her poor head that if her little girl had lived she would have grown up exactly like you."

"The Comberford girls thought I was like Lady Brookstone," said Nelly musingly. "Mayne was vexed with them for saying so."

"I am afraid Mayne is very easily vexed. The resemblance really does exist; but it is slight. If it comforts that poor mother to fancy that you are like her lost child, why should we not humour her?"

"Why not, indeed?" said Nelly indignantly. "I liked her from the first; she was so soft and sweet and kind. Of course I would not grieve Mayne for all the world; but I think he is unreasonable about Lady Brookstone."

"Extremely unreasonable. And if you yield to him he will grow worse and worse."

Punctually at four o'clock on Wednesday afternoon Nelly presented herself at Lord

Brookstone's bright little house in Park Lane. It was not, of course, in apple-pie order; there were trunks and packing-cases in the hall; the drawing-room furniture had gone into brown holland for the winter; but in Lady Brookstone's boudoir there was warmth and beauty and light.

The room was one harmonious glow of rich red, for the mistress of the house loved sumptuous colours at all times. To-day when chilly mists were gathering in the park, and the trees were fast losing their last sere leaves, the warm tints here were welcome to Nelly's eyes. She, too, revelled in this ruby light and shade. The roselights in the middle of the room deepened into a ruddy darkness in the nooks and corners. Lady Brookstone, rising out of her velvet chair by the fire, came forward to meet her visitor.

"You must sit here, where I can look at you," she said half playfully, but there was an

expression of intense tenderness in her eyes.
"Does it not seem a long time ago since I
first saw you, lying on the couch at Rosedown?
I have been thinking of you ever since that
day."

"And I," answered Nelly softly, "have
thought a great deal of you."

The elder woman bent towards her eagerly.

"Ah," she said, "if only we could spend a
longer time together! I want you to tell me
all about yourself, and the first things that you
can remember. Do you think it strange that
I should take so much interest in you?"

"It surprised me a little," Nelly begun; and
then hesitated and paused.

"Lady Florence has told you something,
has she not?" Lady Brookstone asked quickly.
"You are like my lost child; you have looks
that she had; her eyes are yours. And there
is a resemblance to me in your face. We are
alike in expression; our voices have the same

tone. Lord Wyburn noticed this, and spoke of it to my husband."

Again the guilty blush dyed Nelly's cheek. "The dark ladye" smiled, and lightly touched that smooth cheek with the tip of her finger.

"You have made a conquest, little one; but I must not talk about it, must I? That tall lover of yours with the blue eyes already scents danger when I approach you. Are you very much in love with him? It is an impertinent question, I know."

It would have been impertinent from any other lips; but Lady Brookstone asked it with that sweet subtle smile of hers, and Nelly could not take offence.

"Yes; I am very much in love with him," the girl replied frankly. "And it is good of him to love me, a poor little nobody, quite alone in the world."

Just one gleam of fire shot from beneath "the dark ladye's" jetty lashes.

"You do not know that you are a nobody," she said, in a voice that she forced to be calm. "He has lighted on a gem that a prince might be proud to wear. Don't let those people at Hartside undervalue you!"

"I could hardly expect them to be pleased with me," Nelly answered sadly. "He comes of a good old family, while I—well, I am a gipsy, I suppose."

"What if you are a gipsy?" Lady Brookstone asked. "Does not the blood of the Romany mingle with families to whom the Comberfords are nobodies? I should like to teach those Hartside people a lesson."

"Oh, they are kind," Nelly said quickly. "And Susie and Phyllis Comberford are really fond of me. They have had troubles and lost money. It is not surprising that they should have wished Mayne to marry well."

"Ah, I heard that they were poor. And the engagement is likely to be a long one.

There will be time for them to find out your true value," Lady Brookstone remarked, with the sweet subtle smile coming back. "Here is my husband. He is most anxious to be introduced to you."

Lord Brookstone was a delicate-featured man, below middle height, with a look of enthusiasm about his beautifully-chiselled face. His eyes were light hazel; full, speaking eyes that changed and softened in a moment; and his hair and silky beard were of that bright red-brown which Raphael loved to paint. At the first glance you would have set him down for what he was, an artist; but you would scarcely have remembered the fact that he was a peer. Sweet-natured, open to all good influences, full of poetry and tenderness, Leonard, Lord Brookstone had escaped many of the snares of a roving life; but at heart he was a Bohemian still.

Asked what would content him he would

answer now as in the old days, to wander on the Continent, to see old towns, and discover rare works of art in odd nooks and corners, to remain a traveller all his life, and be free from those duties and responsibilities of rank which are apt to grow hideously commonplace.

Yes; Lord Brookstone was unquestionably a Bohemian.

CHAPTER XVI.

IN PARK LANE.

A woman perfect as a young man's dream,
  And breathing as it seemed the nimble air
Of the fair days of old, when man was young
  And life an Epic.
LEWIS MORRIS.

NELLY went back to Russell Square in a state of pleasant excitement. Lady Brookstone's delight in her had been so plainly shown that the girl's

heart was moved. They had made her promise to come again on Saturday morning, as
Lord Brookstone wanted to make a sketch of
her. Could she be spared?

Yes; the children might have a whole holiday,
Lady Florence replied. They had been so good
and industrious that they deserved a little re-
laxation. Any one who had been closely observing Lady Florence just then, would have
seen a mischievous twinkle in her eyes; but
this was lost upon Nelly.

The light of that autumn morning stole
softly into the studio in Park Lane. Nelly sat
close to an old china bowl full of large violets,
her hands folded loosely in her lap, her eyes
resting dreamily upon a landscape on the
opposite wall. The soft light and sweet perfume had lulled her into a mood of lazy
content.

She made a lovely picture as she sat there.

" Round the lips a smile
Subtle and sweet and deep as hers who
    looks
From the old painter's canvas, and
    derides
Life and the riddle of things."

Lord Brookstone, happy in his work, sketched
rapidly, finding his task an easy one. His
wife, standing by his side, watched his progress
with an interest so intense that it deepened
the colour in her cheeks.

So the morning slipped away till it was past
twelve o'clock. Nelly had talked and laughed,
but she was so comfortable that she still retained
her pretty pose. Some one who opened the
door saw her sitting in a high-backed oak
chair, with the violets by her side.

It was Lord Wyburn, who had come on
purpose to feast his hungry eyes upon this girl.
Brookstone had run up against him in Bond
Street, and had said that Miss Stanley was

coming to the studio. Lady Brookstone smiled upon him graciously; Nelly met him with tolerable composure, although her heart throbbed with something like fright. What would Mayne say? And yet there was a delicious thrill of gratified vanity.

Wyburn remained to luncheon of course, thus adding fuel to the flame which already consumed him. He had been getting terribly bored with his life of late. It might be possible to live more pleasantly if he were to settle down with this bright face by his side. Nelly was never bored; she enjoyed everything in a fresh girlish way. Surely the worn-out, used-up old world might grow new and rosy were this sweet contagion of enjoyment always present! She was engaged; but somehow he never permitted the thought of her engagement to check his fancy.

On the evening of the same day, Lord Brookstone sauntered into his wife's boudoir after dinner, and found her sitting on a footstool before the fire. She often sat thus, with her hands clasped about her knees, gazing deep into the red glow of the embers.

Something in her face and attitude recalled a time long gone by, and he stood looking down at her in silence for a few moments. Out of the past there arose a vision of a slight, black-haired girl, sitting alone by a fire made of sticks, on the edge of a woody hollow. In the background a red sunset was burning behind a fir plantation; the evening air was sweet with the scent of the woodlands; the tinkle of sheep bells sounded far away. As he drew near, the girl lifted her face; he looked upon its magnetic beauty for the first time; and

> "Felt that light of her eyes into his life
> Smite on the sudden."

And for him those eyes still kept their light,

and the dark, rich face had not lost a single charm.

He sat down in his wife's low chair, put his arm round her, and drew her close to his heart.

"Lost in a reverie, Ursula?" he said.

She nestled close to him, and raised her lips to meet his kiss.

"Leonard, she must be our child." Her sweet voice shook with earnestness. "Let me go over the old story again. It comforts me, and it won't bore you, will it?"

"No, dear, it won't bore me," he answered kindly. "But it saddens me to feel that you are always grieving. And you know that we have no means of finding out the truth, since Abigail is dead."

"It all came to pass because I was fond of Abigail," Lady Brookstone continued mournfully. "When we are true Romany we are faithful; and Abigail and I were more like sisters than cousins. I was an orphan, you know; and my father's sister and her husband were kind to me, as you have heard me say a thousand times. Until you came among us, Leonard, there was never a bitter word between Abigail and me."

"Love's sweetness seldom comes without sowing the seeds of bitterness, Ursula. Abigail was jealous; there are jealous women everywhere; in palaces as well as in gipsy-tents."

"She was a strange girl always; silent and secret as the grave," Lady Brookstone went on. "It all comes back to me as if it had happened only yesterday,—our marriage, and our wanderings, and our settling down for a time in the cottage in Kent. It was there that Abigail and I met again, and she overwhelmed me with her caresses, and her words of false love."

She paused, and he felt her trembling in his arms.

"I know, now, that she must have been false through it all. Our good landlady at the cottage did not like her visits; but you were away abroad, and I was at home with baby alone. It was pleasant to talk with Abigail about old days, and she cheered me in my solitude."

Lord Brookstone touched his wife's forehead with his lips, and stroked her hair tenderly.

"Must you go on, dear?" he asked.

"Oh, Leonard, I cannot help going on! You remember that you had been sent out to the Cape to make sketches for the *Illustrated Argus;* and I was expecting your return when I saw that awful paragraph in the paper. It was rumoured, you know, that some of the men of the Expedition had been killed, and your name was in the list. Can you wonder that I did not stop to reflect? I left baby in the care of Mrs. Fryer, and went up to London to see your old friend Hartland. If any one could help me, Hartland could. He did help me; he found out that the rumour was false, and set my heart at rest."

"Dear Ursula, I wish you would spare yourself!"

"When I came back to the cottage I found Mrs. Fryer awaiting me with a troubled face. Abigail had come in my absence, and had coaxed baby, until the child clung to her neck, and would not leave her. She had always a power of winning children. And baby liked her dark face because it was like mine."

"Not as beautiful as yours, Ursula; not half as beautiful as yours."

"Abigail went away with the child, saying that she would return in an hour. But she had not returned; and I, half crazed with a sudden fear, went in search of her. I found the pateran. I walked and walked until I came to the tents; my people were kind to me in their fashion; but Abigail was not there. That night I stayed with them; but Abigail never came."

She sighed wearily.

"Oh, Leonard, you will never know what I suffered in the days that followed. News came at last that Abigail had joined some of our tribe in Oxfordshire. She went to them quite alone and seemed so ill that a doctor was sent for. But her heart was diseased, they said; and she died in a few hours. That was how it all ended. There was no trace left of my child."

"My poor darling," said Lord Brookstone softly, "it all happened years ago, and heaven only knows what became of the little one. My heart will never cease aching for her, Ursula; but there are some good things in our life that are not taken away. We have each other and our boys."

"Yes," she answered, clinging to him, "yes, I know that I ought to be grateful and glad.

But, Leonard, this girl,—how lovely she is! And they have called her Stanley!"

"That is only because they supposed that she was a gipsy. It does not prove anything, Ursula; as a matter of fact nothing can be proved at all. She may be anybody's child; but it seems to me that they ought to have kept the clothes she wore when she was found. If they had done this there might have been a clue to her parentage. But they did not preserve any relic of her babyhood, and it appears that the woman who adopted her was so well pleased with her toy that she did not want to part with it."

"We were very poor in those days. I could not afford to buy fine clothes for baby; and she grew so fast;" Lady Brookstone murmured. "Leonard, don't you see Nelly Stanley's resemblance to me?"

"She has a look of you, Ursula; there's the same sweet, slow smile. In fact she is the

only woman who has ever smiled as you do,
I think."

"She is our child; I am certain of it. If
we asked her, would she not come to us?"

"I don't know that she would come," Brookstone answered thoughtfully. "She's engaged,
you see. Her future life is pretty well mapped
out."

"But if she is our own—" Lady Brookstone
began excitedly. Her husband stopped her in
his gentle fashion.

"We have not the slightest proof that she
is. Indeed, I don't know why we should cherish
such a notion. If we ask her to live with us,
Ursula, we must accept young Comberford.
He's a decent fellow enough, but you didn't
take a fancy to him."

"No; he didn't like me, Leonard. And he
seemed hard and cold."

"Probably it was Wyburn who hardened
and chilled him." Lord Brookstone laughed

to himself. "After all, Ursula, this Comberford has fairly wooed and won her, you know.
We mustn't interfere. It's unlucky to meddle
in love-affairs, my dear."

CHAPTER XVII.

SHADOWS.

Oh, the little more, and how much it is!
　And the little less, and what worlds away!
How a sound shall quicken content to bliss,
　Or a breath suspend the blood's best play,
And life be a proof of this!
　　　　　　ROBERT BROWNING.

OCTOBER was keeping all its mellow beauty
unimpaired to the last. Sunday came again,
calm and still; but Mayne woke up that morning with a strange unrest within him which
was not to be soothed by the sunshine.

He sat down to breakfast with Mr. Cottrell

as usual, in the pleasant room overlooking Lincoln's Inn Fields. The old man gave him a penetrating glance now and then, and broke a long pause with an abrupt question.

"When will you bring Miss Stanley to see my curiosities, Mayne? Will to-morrow afternoon suit her?"

"I dare say it will," young Comberford answered. "Lady Florence Camden is a good-natured woman; she lets Nelly have plenty of liberty."

"Then bring her here to-morrow at half past three. What's the matter with you, Mayne? You look gloomy this morning."

"Do I?" The young fellow passed his hand across his brow as if he tried to brush a cloud away. "Well, I'll be candid and admit that I am gloomy. I feel as if something were going to happen; and, like Desdemona, I'm haunted by an old song. It was a song that poor Angela used to sing——

"'For violets pluck'd the sweetest showers
  Will ne'er make grow again.'"

"A doleful ditty," said Mr. Cottrell, "yet true enough, Mayne, true enough. As you get older, my boy, you'll find that life's path is strewn with plucked violets. But keep up your heart; you are young, and flowers are plentiful."

"Do you believe in presentiments?" Mayne suddenly asked.

"I've known them to come to nothing," the old man replied evasively. "You are out of sorts this morning; the fall of the leaf has touched you, that's all."

As Mayne came out into Lincoln's Inn Fields he caught sight of Nelly and the children, and overtook them with a few rapid strides. They all passed through the gate together, and heard the cooing of the pigeons as they walked towards the chapel. It struck Mayne that his lady-love was a little quieter than usual; but Louie was loquacious.

"Oh, Mr. Comberford, do you know that Miss Stanley sat for her portrait yesterday?" cried the forward little girl. "She went to Lord Brookstone's studio in Park Lane. Aunt Flo says the picture will be exhibited next year."

"I did not hear of that arrangement," said Mayne, looking steadfastly at his betrothed.

Nelly did not like that look. His eyes were cold and reproachful, she thought, and reminded her of his mother's. What harm had she done that he should regard her with a disapproving gaze?

"There was no arrangement," she rejoined quietly. "It was a sudden idea of Lady Brookstone's. Her husband wanted to please her, I suppose, and asked me to give him a sitting."

"I thought I had mentioned my dislike to your acquaintance with——" he began. Then, observing that Louie was looking profoundly interested he stopped abruptly.

"C—c—coming to tea with us this after-noon?" inquired Robby, plucking at his coat sleeve.

"Yes, of course he is coming." Nelly lifted her eyes to her lover's gloomy face, and gave him one of those wooing smiles which the heart of man can seldom resist. Softened, yet still perturbed in spirit, Mayne followed her into the chapel.

For a little while he had her all to himself in the afternoon. They sat together by the fire in the cosy breakfast-room, and he listened to her soft explanation of yesterday's doings.

Was it her fault, she asked, if Lady Brook-stone would call on Lady Florence? Could she help it if they sent for her to come into the drawing-room?

"I'm only a poor little governess, Mayne," she pleaded in a dulcet murmur. "I have to do as I am told, you see. Other girls can do as they please;—Miss Payton, for example, is her own mistress. If you had got engaged to her she would not have displeased you as I do."

"I never thought of getting engaged to her," he answered.

"But your mother thought of her for you. Oh, Mayne, I sometimes feel that I am a wretched little creature! Have I not spoiled the plans of your family, and made you disappoint everybody?"

He drew her into his arms, and murmured words of comfort after the time-honoured fashion of lovers. She was so tender and sweet, and withal so humble, that he did not care to ask any more questions about the Brookstones just then.

A little later she mentioned carelessly that they were going away to Rome, and would have forgotten her long before they came back.

Not until he was alone again, and she was no longer near to enchant him with her witcheries, did his vague doubts and fears return. They came flocking back to his mind like birds of ill omen, scared away for a time from some favourite haunt; and his whole life was darkened by their presence.

Mr. Cottrell received Nelly, on Monday afternoon, with an old-fashioned courtesy which won her goodwill at once. He was growing old; but when his gaze rested on her beautiful face, his mind skipped nimbly back to the days when he was a young lover, like Mayne, and forgot the working-day world in looking into a pair of brown eyes. He knew that the Comberfords were not overjoyed at the engagement; but this face, he thought, was sufficient excuse for any man's folly.

But was there any folly in the matter? What was more certain to bring out the good in a young man's nature, and subdue the sensual, than——

"The maiden passion for a maid"?

Old Cottrell had watched the progress of

many a love-affair, and it was his deliberate opinion that every mortal who has truly loved another has always been benefited thereby. Whether love ends in a marriage-chime or a dirge, it is still the noblest and purest thing in life. Whether it be crowned with myrtle or cypress it is still the angel that blesses us, and leads us upward into purer air and clearer light.

"You must come into my study to see my curiosities," said Mr. Cottrell, sweeping back the heavy curtain which masked the doorway between the two rooms. "It is not often that my dull sanctum is visited by so bright a guest."

The study presented, in truth, a gloomy aspect. The oaken book-cases had their lower shelves filled with rows of gigantic folios and quartos; and between two of them hung a tall, narrow looking-glass in an antique frame. Confronting the glass was the half-length portrait

of a man attired in the sumptuous costume of
James the First's time. The face, melancholy
and proud, seemed familiar to Nelly, as the
light of the autumn day fell softly on the picture.

"It is the Duke of Buckingham," said Mr.
Cottrell, following her glance. "The portrait
hangs opposite to this glass, in which (if tradi-
tion speaks truth) he once strove to read his
future fate. The glass—you see it has an ancient
frame—is believed to have belonged to Lilly
the astrologer; and its dim surface once reflected
the phantoms which he summoned from the
world of shadows."

Nelly turned to look at the "magic mirror,"
and saw in it only the reflection of her own
lovely face, with cheeks richly glowing, and
brown eyes shining. She shook her head at
the bright image with a smile.

"It shows me nothing worse than myself,"
she said gaily. "I wonder if Buckingham
caught a vision of Felton's knife?"

"If he had seen it he might have escaped it," Mayne remarked.

"I think not," Mr. Cottrell replied. "It is seldom that a man accepts a warning. But here is something prettier for Miss Stanley to see."

He unlocked the door of an ebony cabinet, and took out a round, flat case. Opening this, he displayed a delicately-painted miniature of a fair woman, with little rings of light hair curling on her forehead, and a string of pearls round her slender throat. The mild blue eyes looked meekly into Nelly's brown orbs; the dainty lips wore a faint smile.

"Do you recognize her?" the old man asked. "Poor Louise—best, and unhappiest, of all the favourites of Louis the Fourteenth's court! See this curl of light hair, fair and soft as a child's; it was shorn from her head when she assumed the habit of a Carmelite."

He showed the curl, encased in glass at the back

of the miniature; and Nelly looked at it intently. Then she turned to the fair face again, studying it long with an earnest gaze, as if it fascinated her.

"Does it speak to you?" said Mr. Cottrell after a pause. "It has often spoken to me. It seems to say—'I am a woman with a vast capacity for loving. I love unlawfully, with a deep voice within my soul condemning this wild devotion. I know that the time will come when my king will grow weary of my love; and even now—

'The shadow darkens round me of my fate;
   I hear the choir upon the midnight swelling,
There closes on me the eternal grate
   Where banished and forsaken hearts are dwelling.'

"This is the kind of love that ends in the convent, Miss Stanley. La Vallière was a fool, was she not?"

"A fool of whom one thinks tenderly," Nelly answered with a little sigh.

"Now look at this,"—Mr. Cottrell took out a fan, exquisitely painted—"see these smiling cupids hovering over a rose-crowned goddess! The fan belonged to poor Louise's rival, Madame de Montespan. And here is a little bonbon box which the Grand Monarque used to carry in his august pocket. These turquoises are very fine."

Nelly took the little box in her hand, and examined it with all a woman's delight in pretty trifles. But Mayne was growing impatient for something more interesting to be exhibited.

"These things are all very well, Mr. Cottrell," he said. "But your crystal—ah, that's the best of all!"

CHAPTER XVIII.

THE CRYSTAL.

Look, look again ere the moment pass!
One shadow comes but once to the glass.
DANTE G. ROSSETTI.

"THE crystal? Will nothing else content you,
Mayne?" the old man asked. "I have trinkets
and baubles enough here to amuse Miss Stanley
the whole afternoon."

"But I have told her about the crystal,"
Mayne answered. "How you brought it from
India, and how it was said to have been used
in divination. Nelly is longing to look into it."

"Are you willing that she should look into
it?" Mr. Cottrell demanded.

"Willing? Of course I am." The young
fellow laughed outright. "I've looked, myself,
a dozen times at least without seeing anything.

If she has no better luck than I have had, she will be disappointed."

"Let me look," pleaded Nelly, in her sweet voice. "Perhaps I shall see more than he did; who knows?"

"Ay, who knows?" echoed Mr. Cottrell, turning to the ebony cabinet once more.

Carefully selecting one small key from his bunch, he unlocked a drawer, and took out a bag of wash-leather. Then, with a cautious hand, he drew forth a ball about the size of a Mandarin orange; a thing so transparent and purely bright that it looked like a huge dewdrop.

Nelly received the ball eagerly in her pretty little fingers. She turned it over and over, looking as pleased as a child with a new toy.

"Let the light fall upon it," said Mayne. "Sit here, in this easy-chair, with your back to the window. That's right. Now gaze steadily into the crystal for ten minutes."

"Ten minutes? That's rather a long time."

"It will be good discipline for you," Mayne declared. "There's too much quicksilver in you, Nelly. We must all be perfectly silent."

"And you must be very much in earnest," said Mr. Cottrell. "Desire to see with all your might."

The beautiful face grew suddenly grave and intense; the smile died away from the soft lips.

There was no sound to break the stillness which reigned in the room; the noises in Lincoln's Inn Fields were heard but faintly here; and Mayne, who had flung himself into a chair, remained quite motionless, watching his betrothed so fixedly that he did not bestow a single glance upon his godfather. The old man stood resting one arm on the mantelpiece, and looking intently at the girl. His eyes, usually placid and dull, were now bright with a fiery light. A clock, on its bracket in a corner, ticked the time away; but only seven minutes had passed when Nelly suddenly uttered a little cry.

"What is it? Did you see anything?"
Mayne asked springing up from his seat.

She let the crystal drop into her lap, and
looked up at him with a bewildered air. The
colour was gone from her cheeks, and her
brown eyes, heavily fringed by the black lashes,
shone out strangely. Old Cottrell passed his
hand across his face, and moved quietly away
from the fire-place.

"Have you had enough of this thing, Miss
Stanley?" he asked, taking the transparent ball
out of her lap. "The vision only comes once,
you know, and then but for a moment."

He spoke in a half-playful tone, and held the
crystal carelessly in his hand. No one would
have supposed from his manner that he thought
seriously of the matter; but Nelly shivered
slightly when he spoke.

"I don't want to look into it any more,"
she answered in a subdued tone.

"Did you see anything?" Mayne repeated.

" You foolish child, I believe you are scared! What was it that you fancied you saw?"

" It was mere fancy." She sat upright, giving a light touch to the folds of her pretty dress.

" But tell us what the fancy was," he insisted.

" Why?" she demanded, with a little laugh.

Already she had regained her self-control, although the rich rose-flush had not come back to her cheeks. She picked up the grey gloves she had been carrying, and had laid down on a table near her. And in picking up those little kid gloves she seemed to have taken up again the manner she usually wore, bright, yet gentle, and entirely self-possessed.

" You want to laugh at me," she went on, straightening the fingers of the little gloves with dainty touches. " You want to taunt me with my imaginative temperament. For the rest of my life I am to be derided as a silly, nervous creature, given to seeing visions, and dreaming day-dreams!"

She drew her breath quickly, but her face

had lost the blanched look, and the usual soft languor had come back to her eyes. Old Cottrell regarded her quietly, and secretly admired her courage.

"You gave a little scream, you know," said Mayne.

"Did I? That was just one of my pretences. I like to make a sensation now and then."

"I think you are pretending now," Mayne said, almost angrily, "that you were not frightened, —why, Nelly, I saw terror in your face!"

"Do you really suppose that I saw a scaffold, or a skeleton?" she inquired coolly.

"I don't know what you saw; but I know you were frightened," he answered stubbornly.

Mr. Cottrell opened the drawer in the ebony cabinet again.

"The crystal shall go back to its hiding-place," he said in his quiet voice. "It has done mischief enough for one day;—it has made something like a quarrel between a pair

of true lovers. Ill-omened thing, thou shalt
see the light no more!"

"But it takes two to make a quarrel," cried
Nelly softly. "And I have no mind for strife.
Isn't it a pity to waste any more of this pleas-
ant afternoon in an idle dispute?"

She glanced at Mayne with all the old
witchery in her smile.

"The tea-pot is cooling in the next room,"
said Mr. Cottrell, turning the key in the drawer,
shutting up the cabinet, and then putting his
hand on his godson's shoulder. "I am a
stupid old fellow for keeping a witch's tool in
my possession, and letting young people handle it.
No good ever comes of nonsense of this kind."

"Of course it is nonsense," Mayne replied
irritably. "And if Nelly would only tell what
she thought she saw, we might——"

"But I was dazed with staring hard at the
thing!" the girl explained. "Oh, Mayne, do
forget all about it, and let me have some tea."

There was no resisting such an appeal as this. Mr. Cottrell laughed good-humouredly, and the three went into the adjoining room, where an antique silver urn was steaming on the table. Nelly's eyes were gladdened by the sight of beautiful old china cups, and a bunch of chrysanthemums in a delicate Venetian vase. All the furniture in this room was pretty and bright; they seemed to have left shadows and gloomy thoughts behind the door of the study.

Yet, although the young people appeared to have regained their cheerfulness, the crystal was not quite forgotten. When Nelly had finished her first cup of tea she admitted that she had felt exhausted.

"The tea did me good," she said, as she handed her cup to Mr. Cottrell. This time she looked frankly up at him, and there was something in those uplifted eyes that touched him.

"I knew it would," he answered.

She smiled, and glanced at Mayne, who was

watching her every movement and change of expression.

"The first chill of autumn has been creeping over me," she said. "What a long time it will be before we see another summer!"

She moved a little nearer to the fire, putting one small foot on the fender, and shivering again.

"Are you cold?" Mayne asked anxiously.

"Yes;—no,—not exactly."

Mr. Cottrell came to her side with another cup of tea, and she took it gratefully. Then there was a brief silence, and both the men saw that she had grown pale again.

"Supposing," she said suddenly, turning to the old man. "Supposing that one really did see something unexpected when one looked into a crystal——" She paused.

"I know what you wish to ask," rejoined Mr. Cottrell, with a glance at Mayne which silenced him. "Let me explain to you a simple theory of mine. Is it not possible that, under certain conditions, the thoughts of our hearts may take visible shape? The thing that we have sometimes dreamed of in secret may haply be presented for a moment to our bodily eyes. And we, startled and confused by this unexpected sight, may be weak enough to believe that it is the picture of a future which can neither be altered nor controlled."

"You hold, then, that a man's future is in his own hands. You despise the word kismet?" said Mayne.

"Kismet!" repeated Mr. Cottrell with quiet scorn. "It is the poorest excuse that a fool ever made for his folly. Has it not been well said that the future is Now? Are we not engaged in daily weaving for ourselves a pattern which shall surprise us one day?"

Nelly had listened to him with earnest attention. Her rich colour came and went softly, and the warm brown light of her eyes was beautiful to see.

"I believe you are right," she said, as she rose from her chair. "Mr. Cottrell, I have had a delightful afternoon, and I shall remember your words."

She held out her hand to him, giving him a clear, candid look and smile. Presently the door had closed upon herself and her lover, and their host was left alone with the empty tea-cups and the fire.

He sat down in the low easy-chair which she had occupied, and looked out, with dreamy eyes, into the gathering twilight. From his seat he could just see the tops of the tall trees in Lincoln's Inn Fields, swaying now in that soft chilly wind which comes sometimes with an autumn gloaming.

Mr. Cottrell was a man who had preserved, through a retired and studious life, a heart still easily touched by any episode of a senti-mental kind. He saw, or thought he could see, that the girl was incapable of making an

adequate return for her lover's love. Was
it her fault if she gave him mock pearls for
his pearl of great price?

After all, was not Mayne Comberford a
lucky fellow to have won this bright creature,
with her witcheries and her surpassing beauty?
Would there ever come a time when he would
turn to her for something more than it was in
her power to bestow? Old Cottrell knew
some of the secrets of married lives. He knew,
only too well, the anguish of that supreme
moment when one makes the first discovery
of inequality. It is a discovery that many
women have made, and have lived on as good
wives and mothers till the close of their days.
It is a discovery that many men have made,
and have resolutely set themselves to the task
of being good husbands and fathers till their
journey's end.

But what if there should be no marriage at
all between these two?

"Then he would suffer," mused the old man by the fire. "And he would find out that suffering can produce strange changes in the inner life. He is a man who will never know what lies within him until he has lived through a heart-sorrow. It is to him who eats the bitter herb that strength is given;—strength which can be drawn out of the bitter, but never out of the sweet."

The grey shadows darkened, and filled the room in which old Cottrell sat alone. He sank back in the arm-chair, and closed his eyes, passing tranquilly from his reverie into a quiet sleep.

The housekeeper, coming in to light the lamps, gently roused him from his slumber. A few minutes later Mayne came bounding upstairs, happy and vigorous. Nelly had found a means of charming his dark mood away.

END OF VOL. I.

SELECTIONS FROM
MESSRS. HUTCHINSON'S LIST.

BY W. L. REES.

The Life and Times of Sir George Grey.
K.C.B. By W. L. REES. With Photogravure Portraits. In demy 8vo. buckram gilt, 2 vols. 32/-. and in one vol. 12/-.

The *Daily Telegraph* (Leader) says:—"A work of extraordinary interest."

BY DOUGLAS SLADEN.

The Japs at Home. With over 50 Full-Page
and other Illustrations. Third edition. In demy 8vo. cloth, 6/-.

The *Times* says:—"His notes and impressions make capital reading, and we feel on closing the volume that it is not a bad substitute for a visit to Japan."

BY GILBERT PARKER.

Round the Compass in Australia. Demy
8vo. cloth gilt, fully illustrated, 3/6.

The *Pall Mall Gazette* says:—"Mr. PARKER may fairly claim to have produced one of the most readable of recent works on Australia."

BY MRS. OLIPHANT.

The Cuckoo in the Nest. A Fifth Edition.
With Illustrations by G. H. EDWARDS. In crown 8vo. cloth gilt, 6s.

The *Athenæum* says:—"Mrs. OLIPHANT's most successful novel."

BY F. FRANKFORT MOORE.

"I Forbid the Banns." The Story of a Comedy
which was played seriously. Sixth Edition. Cr. 8vo. cloth gilt, 6/-.

The *Athenæum* says:—"So racy and brilliant a novel."

By the author of "I FORBID THE BANNS."

Daireen. A Novel. Second Edition. In
crown 8vo. cloth gilt, 6/-.

BY CLARK RUSSELL.

The Tragedy of Ida Noble. With over
Forty full-page and smaller Illustrations by EVERARD HOPKINS. In crown 8vo. buckram gilt, gilt top, 6/-.

The *Times* says:—"Mr. CLARK RUSSELL has never written a better story than 'The Tragedy of Ida Noble.'"

BY AMELIA E. BARR.

A Singer from the Sea. In crown 8vo.
cloth gilt, 5/-.

BY ANNIE S. SWAN.

A Bitter Debt. A Tale of the Black Country.
With Illustrations by D. MURRAY SMITH. In cr. 8vo., cloth gilt, 5/-.

LONDON: HUTCHINSON & CO., 34 PATERNOSTER ROW.

www.ingramcontent.com/pod-product-compliance
Lightning Source LLC
Chambersburg PA
CBHW030806020726
47499CB00006B/1795